Dear Vidyarthi
Here is from a
stricken heart
about Kashmir.
with warm
regards
from
Uncle Mulk
1995

Death of A Hero

DEATH OF A HERO

Epitaph for Maqbool Sherwani

MULK RAJ ANAND

abhinav publications

Publishers
Shakti Malik
Abhinav Publications
E-37, Hauz Khas
New Delhi-110016

ISBN 81-7017-329-9

Lasertypeset by
Tara Chand Sons
Naraina, New Delhi

Printed at :
D.K. Fine Art Press (P) Ltd.
Delhi-110052

PRINTED IN INDIA

THE POPLARS whirred past him...And they still came towards him, on both sides of the road...Long unending lines of poplars...

But when he thought about it he found that it was actually he who was whirring past them on his motor bike.

The leaves of the trees had been much more green two days ago, when he had fled from Baramula to Srinagar, than they were now in the light of the declining sun, while he was returning from Srinagar back to Baramula.

'Perhaps,' he said to himself in the diffused language of the wordless colloquy within him, 'perhaps I fancy the leaves were much more green because the autumn is a sad season in our land.'

'Or perhaps it is the sunset...'

'Also death—the death of those whom the invaders have murdered!...And fear for oneself!...'

And he became conscious of his increasingly morbid preoccupation with the poet's lament, which was forming on his tongue without becoming fluid, the lament about the possibility of his own death...

As the rutted, straight tarmac road dissolved under the wheels of his 'Triumph,' he had another fateful echo augury in his mind from the days of his childhood in the convent school, the Biblical phrase: 'How sweet for our souls to be borne to the skies, our journey done, our journey done...'

But he felt afraid of the potency of the phrase if it should apply to himself. He looked away.

The wintry sky on this late afternoon, the red sun tinting the snowy clouds above the mountains, and the chill mist covering the shallows and the swamps of the threatened valley, all seemed to bring the shadows nearer. The front was only ten or twelve miles away and yet it was as quiet as in the peaceful village in the middle of the valley.

'La hol billah!' he mumbled the cautionary phrase to calm himself.

He recalled that he had gone through so many emotions during the last three days: the feeling of weakness during the flight from his little home town after the Pakistani raiders had occupied it, the fear that he might not get to Srinagar, the elation of being in that odd room with the others in Amira Kadal, the shock of finding out that those who had begun this sudden invasion, with loot, as soon as they arrived in the villages, were the so called 'Muslim brethren', the utter frustration of the confusion which prevailed in the city: then the mixed exaltation and fear of being chosen to go back to Baramula to rally the people; and, underneath it all, the complete innocence about what would happen to him if the tribesmen were already there...But there was, below the surface, a feeling he did not wish to acknowledge, the sense of chivalry: against tribalism—the genuine human response of pity.

And now, this was more boring than ever, this ride back home, because he could not even think in the state of emotional stress, did not know his destination, or the way to get there if the road was blocked.

The noise of the machine dispelled his confusion, even as it sent the sparrows in the poplars scattering into the chenars in the fields by the road. Only the sights and sounds of the evening landscape filled his senses: bleak, dreary uncultivated fields with the stubbles of the last harvest, the melancholy willows leaning over small pools; the pine forests on the slopes of the mountain, weighted down by dark, ominous clouds on the right above Gulmarg; and the peaks of the mountain ranges standing steel grey in the distance.

There was not a soul stirring on the landscape on either side of him.

Instinctively, he jerked his head up, against fear, as though to rise above the natural humility of his being before reality.

And he decided in his private colloquy that he must go on, once he had decided to go...Things were badly mixed up. But he must go right ahead and not be craven and panicky and confused any more. He was going to Baramula, perhaps to certain death. But the head of the volunteer corps had said to him: 'Maqbool Sherwani—we are in peril! We must do everything to avert the disaster! We must save our people! We must stand by them and each other!...We must resist the butchery with our bare hands!...' Apart from other things, it was the horror of the butchery which had moved him, and his advance into danger became a kind of protest against occupation of Baramula by the raiders.

Somewhere between the impact of these words and his own uneasiness, lay the fear; somewhere, under his skin, in the nerves above the tendons and the sinews of his body, there were uncontrolled tremors, as though the taut muscles were relaxing, and accepting the choice he had made.

Neither he nor his people had provoked this onslaught. And yet they were being punished. But to the poet in him, this seemed always to be so, Allah notwithstanding.

The situation has arisen all in three days, in which every Kashmiri would be tested. Those who believed in God would accept their fate as though it was the trial on judgement day. But those who hoped for a new morning for Kashmir would have to fight, because only through survival would there be a chance to metamorphose the thoughts, opinions and beliefs of the young from the past servility. In such a strange situation, he told himself, the only thing to do was to go on, like a sleepwalker, to transcend the occasion, as though inspired.

Lest his naive resolve seems too heroic to himself, he relaxed the stance of his head from the rigid inclination to the left and looked on to the right.

The rice fields of Pattan were showing up now, tiers of lush green, yellowed here and there by the setting sun where paddy was ripe for cutting. The world of nature engulfed his ardent young poet's spirit. His fondness for the lush vegetation and flowers of Kashmir had always been the nostalgia of a man living with poor arid souls, the heightening produced by the lovely gardens and falling waters, as an escape from his own burning heart. And soon the big village itself stood before him with its wooden houses. He knew it to be as shaky and ramshackle and decaying as Baramula, and dirty, with garbage dumps and smelly little rivulets of drains in the gulleys, but it looked, at this distance, like the picturesque villages of Switzerland, such as the nuns had shown him at school in their photograph albums. The groups of chenar trees on the outskirts looked purple and gold and turquoise in the departing light.

Now he could see a few dim figures crouching by the putrid pond, seemingly women fetching water.

And soon a shepherd was leading his goats and sheep with uplifted stick by the willows on the right hand side of the road.

But the rows of the straggling roadside shops, on the half a mile or so before Pattan, were closed, and congeries of Kashmiris, who usually sat huddled in their cloaks smoking the common hookah, were absent.

This general emptiness betokened the spreading fear of the Almighty, or perhaps, worse still, the actual occupation by the raiders. A drowsy mongrel dog woke up from under the boards of a wayside stall and yelped at the motor cycle.

He slowed down the engine, which backfired noisily and made the dog run abreast of the machine and bark more viciously. This seemed like the proverbial warning from hell, as it sent shivers through his weakening legs.

He decided to pull up Mahmdoo's cookshop, which stood about a hundred yards outside Pattan. If anyone could give him the news, it was Mahmdoo.

But the noise of the motor cycle may create panic. He shut off the engine and free-wheeled along.

The dog snarled away, back to its shelter.

4

The door of Mahmdoo's cookshop was closed. But from the chinks in the rough wooden boards, Maqbool could see a cotton wick earthen saucer lamp lighting the gloom.

'Mahmdoo,' he whispered.

There was no response. Only the flickering light glowed.

'Oh Mahmdoo, Hatto!...It is me—Maqbool Sherwani!'

With his eyes more accustomed to the gloom, as they rivetted into the interior through the chinks, he could now see the huge platform above the earthen oven on which Mahmdoo usually sat, baking hot bread, or stirring the various meats in the cauldrons, or brewing salt tea in the brass samovar.

Maqbool surmised that the shrewd cookshopwallah had accounted discretion the better part of valour, for the place where food was to be had would be one of the first to be visited by the hungry invaders. At least that had been so in the half of Baramula which the raiders had taken before he left...Did this mean that Pattan had been occupied? But there would have been Pakistani sentries all over the place, and certainly on the main road, if they had already reached here...

'Mahmdoo!' he called again.

Not from inside the shop, from behind him, across the road, came a whisper:

'Come this side.'

Maqbool turned round and saw Gula, the young son and assistant of Mahmdoo, in his soiled tunic and salwar, standing by his motor cycle.

'Father is in the sitting room of Pandit Janki Nath,' Gula said. 'He would like you to come there. But, he says, hide the motor cycle somewhere before you come...I will take it to the back of the shop.'

'No, it is heavy and you will fall with it,' Maqbool said. 'I will wheel it there and hide it if you show me the way.'

Gula, excited at the prospect of being able to handle the motor cycle after Maqbool would go up to see his father, went ahead into

5

the alleyway eagerly enough.

The alley was narrow and the energy and the concentration required to manoeuvre the heavy machine up to the doorway of the courtyard brought sweat to his face. Fortunately, the space outside the backdoor was wider. And he negotiated the motor cycle into the small courtyard, full of pitchers and dirty utensils and fuel and all the other muck of the cookshop.

'Don't you tinker with the machine!' he said to Gula with an affectionate smile. 'The motor has a habit of running away.'

The boy who had been itching to handle the machine, docilely followed Maqbool to where his father sat in Pandit Janki Nath Kaul's room.

Mahmdoo got up cordially and shook the right hand of Maqbool with both his puffy hands.

'Hatto, you have grown fatter with doing nothing!' Maqbool greeted him. 'And you are beaming with happiness! Have you been eating up all the food in your cookshop yourself?'

'Maqbool!' Mahmdoo protested at the banter and apologised: 'I can't help my fat body. You know—the oil and butter get into one's skin when one's cooking!....'

'What is the news?'

'Ao!'

'A wonderful carpet and cushions! How did the Pandit trust you not to make them greasy?'

'Sir, when it is a question of life and death, even a money-lender like Pandit Janki Nath can forget about his property...You are a learned man and don't know much about the ways of men. They fled to Srinagar three days ago after they received the news of the death of their relations in Baramula. A little while after you left...'

Maqbool searched Mahmdoo's face. The cookshop keeper obviously thought him to be a useless, unpractical fellow. Perhaps that was true, Maqbool admitted, because he had always seemed so unsure about everything to people. But was there also the insinuation that he was weak like Janki Nath?

6

'You had your own reasons for going to Srinagar, Maqbool Sahib, but they were protecting their skins!...' Mahmdoo said to confirm Maqbool's prognostications.

'Mahmdoo, no one is better than another in the face of death...If I am to confess the truth, I also ran away. And it needed some persuasion to bring me back...'

Against such truthfulness, Mahmdoo could only be silent. And, after a while, he also mustered the necessary courage to speak of his own fears:

'I have closed the shop! The Pakistanis may be here any moment. And they will be hungry and will not spare me...Some half a dozen of them have already arrived at Baramula end of this town and are staying at the Pattan house of Sardar Muhammad Jilani...Now, when will they send up help from Srinagar?'

Maqbool stared vacantly in front of him for a moment. He was unnerved by the news of the nearness of raiders. And he wondered how to explain the position to Mahmdoo without causing him to panic.

'Our people are busy...Strange...I have never seen a Sarkar run like this. They work from a room on top of the Palladium cinema. There they sit and talk, old and young. The wiser heads debate...The young men have formed an army and have collected all kinds of arms. Jawaharlal has condemned Pakistan for helping the Pathan raiders to attack Kashmir...'

'Then we are totally against Pakistan?' Mahmdoo asked.

'To be sure!' answered Maqbool a trifle impatient. 'These are not Muslim brethren, who have come attacking us! If they were brothers, they would have talked to us—not begun to murder us!'

'Sire, far be it from me to suggest anything else, but you know the bazar gossip...'

'To be sure we tried to tell Jinnah to keep off Kashmir. But the exalted butchers, and the white skins behind them, have prepared the invasion. They armed them and sent them in army trucks. They have set up an 'Azad Kashmir' Government in Rawalpindi, with

Muhammad Ibrahim at the head. And they now say we are with them!!!'

Mahmdoo was silent again. The political words of Maqbool Sherwani were too clear to allow him to doubt, though he could not comprehend everything.

'Do you realise what they have done in Baramula? These "Muslim brothers"! In their holy war?' continued Maqbool. 'They have looted both Hindus and Muslims...And they took the shame of women!... They may soon do the same in Pattan!...'

'As Baramula is richer than Pattan, perhaps it will take a few days for them to collect all the loot!' said Mahmdoo, half from wishfulfilment and half out of bitter humour.

'But we can't sit here talking,' said Maqbool suddenly. I must go ahead...'

Mahmdoo dared to look up at Maqbool's face. It was a lean pale face, with the delicate golden broom of youthful fine hair on the upper lip. At once the intelligence of the young man was obvious to the shrewd shopkeeper, but at the same time, the impetuosity and the lack of mature judgement.

'Sire, one does not walk into burning fire,' counselled Mahmdoo. 'One allows flames to die down a little—'

'But if one makes no effort to extinguish the fire it has a way of spreading,' said Maqbool. 'Pattan is not far from Baramula...And, after Pattan, Srinagar is not much further! And they may spread out if they are not stopped at Baramula...'

Mahmdoo could not understand how they were to be stopped at Baramula. Apart from the traditional fatalism of the villager, who had accepted all kinds of tyranny as the inevitable punishment of the poor as the evidence of his guilt in the eyes of Allah, there was the commonsense cunning of the shopkeeper, which was proof against the literate. On the other hand, the Pakistanis were ruffians to send the tribals here, eating up all the chickens. He had heard that there was not one chicken left in Baramula.

'Sire...' Mahmdoo began but could not finish his sentence.

Maqbool understood the man's meaning from the curious intonation of his voice and the pallor on his face.

'I will go now, Mahmdoo,' he said, I will have to leave my motor cycle here...'

This sentence brought a glow on the face of Gula, though it seemed to confuse Mahmdoo.

'But you must have some warm tea,' Mahmdoo said, heightening with the feeling of traditional hospitality due to a man in the cold and the dark. 'Gul, go and make some tea...'

Maqbool would have refused if he had not suddenly become possessed with the sense of his failure with Mahmdoo. What was the use of his going to Baramula to rally people, if he could not convince this man. He sat silent with a bent head seriousness, which compelled Mahmdoo to sympathy.

'Oh! Gul, hurry, son!' Mahmdoo shouted after his son.

'The samovar is nearly boiling, Baba,' Gula said. 'And Babu Ishaq is brewing tea.'

Mahmdoo's face suddenly fell as a fat man's face seldom falls.

'Ishaq is—that teacher—once colleague of mine—in the school at Baramula?' Maqbool asked after a while.

Mahmdoo nodded his head and then after a tense silence said:

'Never trust a cockeyed fellow!'

Hardly had he declared this dictum when Ishaq appeared at the door, a pale, shrivelled up man, cockeyed and, therefore, lacking in the dignity of weakness which somehow surrounds everyone in a village.

'The boy won't take lesson!' said Mahmdoo going up to him by the door in an attempt to put him off the scent and to see if he would go away. 'Gula thinks it is all a holiday...'

Mahmdoo had never been known to be inhospitable. In fact, his cookshop kept an open-door policy and many, who could not afford to buy food, came there and ate without paying. The teacher almost lived on Mahmdoo, eating in lieu of the tuitions he gave to Gula.

As he sensed the coldness in Mahmdoo's voice, Ishaq felt there was some special reason for his words. This made him explore the room. And with his uncanny squint eye, he saw Maqbool Sherwani sitting there.

Extending his right arm to wish Mahmdoo out of his way, he advanced, taciturn and paler than usual towards the stranger. And, with a pat of bonhomie, he uttered a loud greeting:

'Say Maqbool Sahib—have your leaders accepted defeat yet or not?'

Maqbool knew this school teacher to be a fanatical pro-Pakistani.

With an affected air of casual indifference, he answered:

'Ao! Ishaq Sahib...'

Ishaq came and sat down, followed by Mahmdoo whose padded face reflected the worst fears after these men had come face to face with each other.

'Our brethren from Pakistan have completely liberated Baramula,' Ishaq began challengingly. 'And they have spread out in two flanks towards Srinagar. I hear they are attacking the main town from the aerodrome side on the one hand and from Gandarbal side on the other. They have taken the Electric Power House. Srinagar is in darkness tonight. And we expected them to be in Pattan tonight or tomorrow morning.'

'Babu Ishaq, how do you know all this?' Mahmdoo asked, partly because he did not believe that Ishaq could know and partly out of pity for Maqbool Sherwani whose morale would surely break down after this talk.

'Our brothers, in the holy war, have trust in me,' said Ishaq almost in a whispered undertone. 'I did not come to teach Gula. I

10

came to ask you to prepare food for them. Sardar Muhammad Jilani has sent orders that everything be done to welcome them when they arrive in Pattan...' And then, turning his gaze towards Maqbool without seeming to turn that way, he said: 'Join our reception committee, Maqbool Sahib. You will see that your leaders will also accept the inevitable.'

'Never!' answered Maqbool. 'It is a   question of principle. Do we believe in Kashmir first, or religion first?'

'In religion—in the religion of our Prophet (may peace be upon his soul), and of our holy Koran.'

'And when did the Prophet, or the Koran say that brother must kill brother?'

'It is not true that our brothers have done this,' said Ishaq in a shrill voice.

'Babu Ishaq,' put in Mahmdoo. 'But there are rumours from Baramula...'

'And they murdered the troops of General Rajinder Singh, whom they took prisoner at Uri, to a man!' put in Maqbool.

'Against infidels in a holy war, there is no avail!' Ishaq said showing his yellow teeth. 'Have not the Hindu Maharaja, and the Dogras crushed us all this time? We cannot surely join with the Hindus in the defence of Kashmir against our own kith and kin!'

'Against murder—one must join even with Shaitan,' said Mahmdoo with his uncanny wisdom.

'And you people talk of principles,' taunted Ishaq.

'Maqbool Sahib does not say what I say,' said Mahmdoo defending the silent guest.

'Then why does not the worthy Maqbool Sherwani answer?' insisted Ishaq.

'I have seen the raiders in Baramula with my own eyes,' said Maqbool in a husky whisper...' Besides, I am for Kashmir. Not for its usurpation by force, but for its freedom to choose where it wants to go. And Nehru can be trusted more than Jinnah. In Karachi they still rely on foreign friends and—.'

'Lies,' said Ishaq, shaking like the branch of a willow tree. 'And your life will not be safe if you talk like this...'

'Babu Ishaq!' shouted Mahmdoo. 'Maqbool Sahib is my guest.'

'As for you, greasy cookshop keeper!' snarled Ishaq. 'I shall see about you!...' And saying this, he got up and turned towards the door with a peculiar alacrity, nearly running into Gula who was bringing the tea tray.

The boy came and, placing the tray on the floor, began to cry.

'You know your school teacher gets angry very quickly, because he is so thin,' Mahmdoo said to console his son.

Maqbool patted Gula on the head and then said to his host:

'I have brought you trouble.'

'I will bring all the troubles you have brought me, as well as mine own, to you,' he said with a slightly forced humour. 'I and Gula will have to come with you to Baramula now!' He paused for a brief moment to explore Maqbool's face for reassurance, and then began: 'I know a track through the fields. And once we reach the outskirts of Baramula, in the dark we can walk to the house of Juma the baker...He is my cousin...Now drink up the hot tea and let's go. That snake may crawl back here...'

The cold frosty air of the late October night had been thickened by the smoke of burning wooden houses as Maqbool and his two companions pushed with aching feet towards a small haystack about half a mile or so out of Baramula.

For nearly four hours they had struggled forward, through the mud and the slush of the fields. And Maqbool looked haggard and worn with the strain of walking in such terrain with Mahmdoo and Gula. Because, though the talk of Ishaq had converted Mahmdoo from the shopkeeper cynic to the side of the innocents, nothing could eradicate the deep fears aroused in him, by Ishaq's fateful announcements about the expected attack on Pattan by the 'Brethren'. Mahmdoo would mistake every bush to be a tribesman and every heightened beat of the reverberating cricket in the wet fields for machine gun fire. Gula was sleepy and had to be carried in turn by Maqbool and Mahmdoo.

Maqbool too had felt during this journey into the unknown that, at any moment, they may come across sentinels or the advance guard of the raiders, for he too had been affected by Ishaq's words. But he surmised that if they had encircled Pattan, they would already have got them, even though he and Mahmdoo had come through a circuitous path in the fields.

What had actually happened inBaramula since he left he did not know. Perhaps they were under good military leadership. And they were waiting for reinforcements before proceeding further. Or they were cautiously fanning out on the flanks of Srinagar from strategic points, as Ishaq had suggested, to probe the situation and then to attack the capital with full force. If the miracle happened, which everyone in Srinagar hoped for, and the Indian army arrived, then the situation may be saved. Otherwise...

He felt a certain pity for the poor cookshop keeper and his son, to be coming with him on this desperate expedition. Some kind of decision was necessary now about these two.

'I am hungry, Father,' Gula whined even as he crumpled up and lay down at the foot of the haystack.

'Chup! Hatto, be a man!' Mahmdoo rebuked him.

That gave Maqbool a cue. For a moment, he stood there listening to the audible darkness, replete with the sounds of vegetation and distant human voices. It seemed to him as though, with exhaustion, the weight of his body had increased. He sat down and began to speak before Mahmdoo may have the chance to say anything:

'So far we have been lucky, Mahmdoo. And I am grateful for this. I would not have liked anything to happen to you and Gula on the way, as you chose to come with me rather than stay in Pattan. Now I cannot ask you to endanger your lives any more...'

'But what are you saying?' protested Mahmdoo. 'I would rather be with you than cooking for the raiders all night under Babu Ishaq's orders!...And, after I took sides with you, he would surely have betrayed me to the murderers. You don't know Ishaq! He believes he is a great man, because he is a school teacher...'

Warm breath issued out of Mahmdoo's mouth in wisps of smoke as he sat by Maqbool and spoke these words. And his peculiar devotion, born through chivalry of the host, which had made Mahmdoo come so far, overflowed into space. Maqbool was sure that though he could not see the face of his companion, there would be tears in the cook's eyes. He would feel lonely, when the father and son would leave him, as he had now decided they must. The wheel of time was turning in his brain and he felt he must turn with it.

'You came with me!' he began in a gentle whisper, 'because my presence with you forced you to take my side in the argument with Ishaq. You would have cooked for Ishaq and his friends out of sheer necessity. I cannot expect you to face possible death for something you may not understand. Perhaps, tomorrow, after you have been in Baramula, you may know what I mean. Even I ran away to Srinagar, thinking everything was lost in Baramula. But I have come back, because I believe help will come to us. I do not want you to stay with me tonight—'

'Sire!' Mahmdoo protested.

'No, if you believe in me, you will have to obey my orders,' said Maqbool sharply. 'You can do something for me. By then you will have time to think and become stronger in your faith. You take Gula to Juma's house. In the morning, if you think the road is clear, send

14

Gula to me here with a message...This plan has to be carried out. Otherwise, all three of us will die dog's death...'

Mahmdoo had no words against this logic. Besides, the suggestion to go met the curve of his own inner desire for safety. Maqbool had guessed rightly.

'I would like to sleep here by Gula—but if you say I must go, I will go...' Mahmdoo said by way of apology.

'If anything happens to me,' Maqbool said, 'Gula can take that motor cycle I have left behind your shop. The locksmith's son in Baramula will teach him how to ride it...'

'What inauspicious talk you do!' protested Mahmdoo.

'Go then—'

Mahmdoo tried to lift his son Gula in his arms. The boy was heavy. So Maqbool got up and, raising Gula from the hay bed, put him silently on Mahmdoo's back like a sack. Having once been a coolie, Mahmdoo could carry the weight easier that way.

'May Allah be with you,' Mahmdoo mumbled.

'Send Gula if you can in the morning,' Maqbool repeated his request. And, as the man walked away slowly, he began to scoop out some hay from the stack before making a cave for himself.

As soon as he lay down anyhow, he was filled with warmth for Mahmdoo, who had put himself into this awkward situation.

The hay had been piled up very compactly. He found that the bushels he had detached were only four feet long. And he was uncomfortable as he lay curled up like a baby. So he took another two bushels out from the side.

For a little while, he felt too desolate to go to sleep. It was strange that now, after the heat of the walk had died down in his body, he began to miss the presence of Mahmdoo and Gula and felt lonely— a kind of emptiness tinged with an endless series of anxieties, vague

15

and amorphous, like menacing shadows cast by the captors of Baramula.

But, outside, the wind rushed through the poplars with a cold swish. Instinctively he clung to himself and pillowed his head with his left arm. Now he felt snug and calm and lay listening to the breeze and to the wetness of the earth sucking up its own moisture. And the fatigue of his body rose like the smell of country liquor to his head and he closed his eyes, dissolving his heavy body into the small space around him, and starting off a series of nightmares in his head.

A lengthy exchange of distant rifle and machine gun fire aroused him from the crazed sleep, in which the last broken edges of dreams showed Mahmdoo and Gula as stags goring him with their horns. He lifted his head and listened, stifling the sentiments about Mahmdoo with a deliberate prejudice in favour of the fat shopkeeper. The distant tat-tat-tat of the machine guns increased. And he was filled with the forebodings which had obsessed him all the way from Srinagar. The only machine guns would be in the hands of the Pakistanis, for he had seen the abject dump of crude single-barrelled and double-barrelled rifles which the people's militia had shown him in the store rooms of the Palladium cinema. But the well-equipped Indian army may have come...

He took a deep breath and listened more intently to locate the exact direction where the sound of firing came from. It was on the Gandarbal side of Baramula. Perhaps the raiders were about to attack Srinagar from that flank, in force. Not that he knew anything about how armies fought, but it seemed strange to his youthful mind that they could advance so far on the flanks, leaving their middle undefended. For if an army had moved with him from Srinagar, on or near the main road to Baramula, it could have got behind them in Gandarbal through the tracks from Pattan and cut them off. But

16

they were no fools, the men who had organised this invasion, Generals Gracey and Tariq. And Liaqat and Abdul Qayum Khan dare not have a defeat on their hands, for Jinnah wanted a *fait accompli*, the possession of Kashmir, knowing he could tackle all the moral hullabaloo of the United Nations afterwards. Dr. Taseer, who had come once to persuade Kashmir to accept the blood brotherhood, but who had found them recalcitrant, had said at last with ruthless logic: 'He who has the big stick will have the buffalo!'

If the fighting was on, he must get up and go and do something. He had no right to rest here. If he had any courage, he must be in the fray now.

But what exactly could he do? He could only sound opinion, tell them the news of imminent help from India and wait.

He wondered what the Russian guerillas had done in similar circumstances under Hitler's occupation? Or the people of the French resistance? And now he regretted that he had only heard rumours of what had happened in the war and had read no books. Never had he felt so abject at his lacks as now. Still he knew that this sudden descent of murder on his land was not an act of God, but a planned brutality to cow people down to submit, and resistance to it was the only virtue. Later he must ask questions and learn the things, so necessary for a young poet. He could not even afford the fare to go to a poetical festival in Srinagar, when he was at school before the world war years. His father had been angry, because he could not give him the money he had asked for, and his mother and sister had been giving him cash from their small savings...And yet his spirit (or was it ambition?) demanded more and more until he had begun to believe that he was one of the most selfish men around Baramula. And the torment of this guilt had made him try to cultivate humility for its own sake, and he had drowned himself in political work. Reading the poems of Faiz, Majrooh, Jafri, Sahir, Nadim, from borrowed books: They had certainly heightened his emotions to high pitch. And this was truly romantic. But why were they not in Kashmir?—Except Nadim...

The rifle fire was sustained. And he felt he could not enjoy the luxury of self-pity any more. He must in the absence of any other concrete plans go and reconnoitre the position in Baramula. The cover, which the darkness afforded, would help him. Only Gula would not find him here, if he came in the morning with a message from Mahmdoo, but he knew that the shrewd Mahmdoo would understand. So he crawled out of the haystack and began to shake off the straw from his clothes.

The snow flakes which had obviously fallen during the night seemed to have melted and the land was slushy as he began to trudge in the diminishing pitch dark before twilight. A sharp wind blew and cut through his woollen jacket. He gathered his muffler around his neck and felt like a scarecrow walking along. That was an advantage, because in case he was observed he could just stand and stretch his hands out, though the tribesmen were more sharp-eyed than he gave them credit for...

Now that he was going along he wanted to make certain where he was going.

The smoke, which still arose from the middle of the town, decided him: It would be futile to plunge into Baramula just like that. He must keep afloat on the sea of existence. And, for this reason, it was best for the while, not to yield to the longing for home, but to attend to the bigger anxiety and avoid being caught.

A shiver went down his spine as he realised that he might walk straight into the arms of a Pakistan sentry or be picked off by a bullet from one of the hawk-eyed ones. And, again his body and mind were in the grip of the crisis which had occupied him before he had dozed off in the haystack: Did one grow up just to be ready to be shot? What did it all mean? Where was Allah? These were questions arising from fear. He sensed the tremors inside himself.

18

And, in this agitation, the choice before him became an obsession. He stopped for a moment, his chin uplifted and his eyes exploring an avenue, chafing at himself for his bad nerves. And then he reasoned, almost audibly: 'Fear is the natural humility of man before ugly reality!'

A little way away from the town, he knew, stood the Presentation Convent, where people were perhaps sufficiently near to be in the know of all that had happened in the three days he had been away and sufficiently far to be out of the trouble spots. As Christians and white folk they would be immune. Besides his father's cousin, Rahti, worked as house mother in the hospital and her husband, Salaama, was the watchman of the convent.

Skirting around the fields, so that he could keep out of visible distance from the town, he headed towards an uprise from which he could descend onto the convent, without the risk of being observed.

In spite of the agitation in him, he pretended to be matter of fact as though he had been to the fields for a walk from the convent.

As he sighted the group of buildings of the Presentation Convent, he found the main house smoking.

Footsore and weary from a further trudge after the long walk from Pattan, he felt listless.

He stopped to see things clearly, imagining that, in the deceptive darkness, he was mistaking the smoke of the chimney for fire. Perhaps it was some other building in the nearby town.

But as far as his eyes could peer into the distance, and figure things out, it was, indeed, the main convent house which was smouldering slowly, the smoke rising like a dense morning mist.

He tried to remain calm and absorb the shock, arguing that he did not really feel any emotion or sentiment about a holy place like a mosque, a temple or a convent. But, all the same, he realised that the raiders had sacked this place. He wondered how the Pakistani officers, who knew of the help given to them by the White generals, had allowed the burning of a missionary centre. The marauders seemed to have engulfed not only the town but also the outskirts, as the weeds in the forest engulf the shrubs and flowers.

So his plan to seek safety among the Christians dissolved.

He stood for quite a while wondering what to do next, unable to believe that the Muslim brethren could set fire to a holy place. But the truth smouldered into his brain with the smoke. Clearly this incendiarism had been recently committed.

At last he was encouraged by the view of the standing houses in the convent courtyard to push on.

Gingerly, he advanced towards the hospital side of the convent, in the courtyard of which Salaama and Rahti had a room.

The frost crinkled under his feet and the beautiful frozen bushes made him feel lonely.

He dared not think of danger, or imagine a catastrophe, for he knew that would be the end of him. And he feigned a casual air, deliberately toughening his sinews, tightening his face and stiffening his neck in the process. This made him a trifle theatrical, but he allowed himself this willed artificiality in the interests of morale. The decision to go forward was like crossing the rubicon from fear to courage. Pausing to look before and after, again he saw that the coast was clear. He hurtled down the hillside.

Long before he got to the courtyard of the hospital, he was challenged by the sweeper Fatah, who having asked: 'Who are you?' ran terror-stricken into the servants' quarters in the courtyard.

'Oh Hatto! It is me,' he spoke in whispers loud enough to be heard. But the diffused terror of the invaders possessed Fatah like a ghost. And he was lost to view among the babble of voices in the servants' quarters.

Luckily for Maqbool, Rahti looked out of the iron bars of the back window of her room and recognised him.

'Our Maqbool,' she said to her husband Salaama, who moaned as he awakened from the half sleep into which he had fallen.

Salaama was nearly delirious and looked with bleary eyes, incomprehensively, at his wife, who had been keeping a vigil by him all night.

Rahti went out and brought Maqbool in, quietly, allaying the fears of the other servants, who had come out to their doors and windows to see if this presaged a new attack by the raiders.

'They are all scared,' Rahti began, 'that the Pakistanis might come back. And, to be sure, there is no knowing what they will do next—if the monsters return! They nearly killed him—' And as she uttered the last words her control broke down. A lump came into her throat and her eyes filled with tears.

'Uncle Salaama,' Maqbool said.

Rahti moved her head up and down affirmatively and her demure, housemother's, face lit up with anguish.

'Is he badly hurt?' Maqbool asked as they got into the raised verandah of the servants' barracks.

She stopped outside the door and told him in whispers:

'They shot at him while he was guarding the front gateway. And, praise be to Allah, the bullet just grazed past his skull. But the bone was chipped and he lost nearly a pitcherful of blood. He collapsed. He had been delirious since...And whole day, yesterday, and all night, he has been...groaning...He had just dozed off a little till your coming awakened him...'

Maqbool entered the neat little room with the big bed and came and leaned over Salaama.

'I am sick, sick...' Salaama burbled like a drunkard from a slobbering mouth which he could open with seeming difficulty. 'Sick!...And those sons of the Devil! They murdered little mother...'

'Do not strain yourself!' Rahti cautioned him. 'I shall tell him everything!' And she turned to Maqbool. 'They killed Sister Teresa,

Assistant Mother Superior! Wounded Mother Superior. Relieved themselves in the chapel!...'

Maqbool perched on the edge of the big bed, his face covered with sweat from the terror that arose in him at this news. And he felt ashamed from fear of his prognostications. Or was it his inner timidity, he wondered?

He put his hands into Salaama's and, for a while, there was silence in the room. Then Salaama groaned and moved his head uncomfortably from side to side.

'Why have you come back to this hell?' Rahti said as she turned from where she was lighting the primus stove.

The young man paused to explore the levels of his mind which had been blurred by what he saw before him. And, then, without raising his voice, so that he should not sound heroic, he said:

'We have to resist the monsters...'

Having said this, he felt that some bigger sanction than his own voice was necessary, because inside him he was even now shrinking from the final words he had left unpronounced: 'or die'. So he added:

'Our leaders in Srinagar think that...And if our luck is good, then, already as I talk, Nehru may have gone into action and sent the Indian army to our relief. The Maharaja has joined India. Srinagar was free when I left yesterday afternoon—'

'We heard different tales,' said Rahti impatiently. 'All we know is that Baramula is completely in the grip of Pakistanis! And they are filling their trucks with loot. If only they would leave us alone now and not come back here...Salt tea—or with sugar?...' All her words were shrill except the last ones.

Maqbool felt a constriction in his throat as he tried to react to her despair. And he could not say anything. He merely sat noticing her nervous hands washing the teapot with hot water to get it ready for tea. The valley seemed to him to have become an orchestra of bitter feelings of despair instead of human voices.

'If there is sugar, I will have it with sugar,' he said after all.

'Ya Allah!...' Salaama pronounced the Islamic incantation even as he turned his head from one side to the other. 'Ache is terrible,' he said. 'Ya Allah...Forgive us...But crush those sons of Shaitan, the marauders!...'

Maqbool felt his pulse and knew that Salaama was running high temperature.

'Try not to speak,' Rahti said in her familiar housemother manner.

'O woman!' he burst out, 'how can I forget these sons of Iblis, when they murdered the little mother in cold blood. I want to get up and murder them all...Maqbool, they are beasts!...They have not only murdered Christians, Hindus and Sikhs, but also Muslims...I hope Allah will punish them for this!...This woman has no faith...She neither believes in Allah nor in Shaitan!...Perhaps she believes in Yessuh Messih...' At this he was seized with a fit of coughing and lifted his head, while Maqbool supported his back.

'But is there Allah?' Maqbool whispered, hoping his uncle would not hear. 'Yessuh Messih was a real person and suffered for mankind—was crucified!'

'Here is some tea,' Rahti said to her husband. Her sorrow seemed to have turned into a cynical tight-mouthed hopelessness.

'I will give it to him,' Maqbool said as he took the cup from her.

This caused a tremor of tenderness to go through Rahti and she melted towards Maqbool and thus towards her husband.

'No, I will give it to him,' she said. 'You have your tea. There it is...'

Maqbool got up and yielded his place to her, so that she could help Salaama sip his tea. And, he took up the cup she had poured for him and stood sipping it, even as he looked out of the window at the mountains beyond.

The twilight was reddening, as though in anticipation of the sunrise. And for a moment he felt that nature would overwhelm the thought of the marauders in his head.

'Our people have hearts,' Salaama said taking his mouth away from the cup. 'I wish I could get up...I would teach these ruffians the lesson of their lives!...' He coughed and nearly spilled the tea.

'Drink up your tea first,' Rahti scolded him. 'You haven't the heart to kill a sparrow. So why boast so much! There is no choice for the poor but to suffer like Yessuh Messih...'

'O go away Hatto, go...' he said impatiently and brushed the tea · cup so, that it fell on the floor at Maqbool's feet. 'I am not like others who will not shout,' Salaama continued defiantly. 'I want to fight!...' But he fell back, exhausted by the effort to say his say.

All the three of them were silent for a while. Rahti was angry, but taciturn, with her anxiety for her husband.

'That is what the people of Srinagar are saying,' put in Maqbool, as though talking aloud to himself. 'We will not accept their rule. And we shall defend ourselves—'

'Brave words are not bullets!' said Rahti cynically, but in a soft voice.

Maqbool came and sat by Salaama again for a while. Then he touched his hands in silence and got up.

'Don't run your head into the noose,' Rahti said. 'They must be looking for you. Stay here a while.'

'No, I must go,' said Maqbool grimly. 'I have to go.'

'That path leads straight to hell!' Rahti shouted.

'Go, go Hatto, go!...' said Salaama excitedly as he raised his head again. 'Go...You will find that the heart of your uncle Salaama is in the right place still. Only head is broken.'

'Lie back still,' Rahti ordered.

Maqbool who had stopped to hear Salaama, issued out into the courtyard.

The cover which the darkness had supplied for his descent upon the convent was being removed by the dawn that rose bloodred from the mountains below the eastern sky. The impetuosity that had made him emerge from the safety of Rahti's room soon gave place again to timidity. He feigned an easy natural gait, however, and headed, through a deserted plain, towards the north end of the main street of Baramula, where the big house of the landlord Sardar Muhammad Jilani stood. His head was bent, as though it was weighed down by thoughts of Allah of a pious Muslim. But his eyes were like gaping pits, unable to believe in the desolation of the once alive Baramula.

In this heightened consciousness of the doom which had settled upon his town, he was aware that there were two kinds of people now left, the many like Rahti who were inclined, fatalistically, to accept what had happened, in spite of their detestation of the misdeeds of the Pakistanis, and the few like Salaama and himself, who were selfwilled and were increasingly possessed by the feelings of protest and resistance. There may be others, he felt, who did not know anything of anything, who were merely like innocent jelly cast into the mould of daily habit and the routine life, wrapped up in the symbols of religious negation, a state of benumbed spirituality, or ritualistic five prayers-a-day worship, or mere family loyalty.

Suddenly, he saw some coolies of Baramula by the octroi post, bearing huge boxes and trunks and sacks into the waiting trucks, which was ostensibly the loot on the way out to Pakistan.

He must not be seen near the octroi post, because the police station was near at hand; and once seen by a policeman he, who was known to the law as a notorious rebel against the Maharaja's rule, would be done for. And yet the mansion of Sardar Muhammad Jilani was at this end of the town.

Anyhow, what guarantee was there that he would be any safer in that house, because, if the information that Babu Ishaq had given him in Pattan was correct, the big landlord of Baramula was acting as the head of the fifth column. Ghulam was at his best, a callow, spoilt child, irresponsible, weakwilled and impressionable in the extreme. It was true that he had given money for the struggle against

Maharaja Hari Singh, but his fear of his father may have dammed up his rebellious sympathies, unless he was still under the influence of his business partner, Muratib Ali. But as against Muratib, there would be the more powerful voice of the ambitious little lawyer, Ahmed Shah, who, Maqbool had heard, had gone over to the Pakistanis. But Ghulam was also his friend, who listened to poetry.

He changed his direction back towards the convent. And, taking cover behind a broken tonga, which stood deserted in the clearing before the congested town, he tried to deliberate on his strategy.

As soon as he stopped, however, all thoughts seemed to fly away from his head, and he had left to him only a beating heart.

It was queer how, when one paused on one's way anywhere, fear seemed to become almost concrete, a kind of undesirable electric shock sent into the body by each sight and sound. He tried to stare at fear itself.

The tonga—had it been broken by the raiders? And were there any Pakistanis in the stables beyond there?

He applied his ears to listen to the possible neighing of horses, but there was dread silence.

His loneliness gripped him, until he had to cough deliberately to relieve the tension.

He must begin to walk, but whither?

The answer came: Muratib Ali was the safest bet. Also, his own house was near Muratib's.

The thought of going nearer home was exciting like the prospect of Muratib's past generosity. For however shallow the opinions of this businessman, his heart could be depended upon. The thing was to get there without being challenged, or without running into someone who may recognise him...There was an approach to

26

Muratib's house from his own lane.

But the dangerous distance to be crossed was the footbridge across the river to the main bazar near his own house.

An alternative course was to get to his own lane, from the dry pond in the fields to the east of the town, by wading into the river half a mile further back on the Pattan road.

He began to walk and this activity dissolved the enveloping anxiety to an extent.

He had not gone far when cries of 'Allah ho Akbar! Allah ho Akbar!' rent the air from the side of the octroi post.

Obviously, it was the Pathan raiders. And he felt it was a wise decision on his part not to go into the main bazar. But, perhaps, if they were concentrated in this area, he had the chance to steal across the footbridge across the river to his own lane.

The resonant praise of Allah repeated itself, but the tone in which it came spread an involuntary chill into his soul. It was fear in the worst sense because it made him shiver. He paused to control himself, to prevent the feeling from becoming obsession of cowardice.

'Maqbool!...' he mumbled to himself.

A vague apprehension of the distance, through which he would have to expose himself on the open bridge, came to him. In order to avoid such exposure and master his fear before it could become cowardice, he decided, on the spur of the moment, that he should go back to the haystack.

He had barely turned when he knew it was far away now.

Rahti's bicycle was the kind of vehicle which would do the trick.

And without much thought of whether Rahti would permit him to use her cycle, he began to walk back.

As he proceeded back towards the convent, absorbed in the sheer physical effort, there was a slight disturbance among the leaves of a chenar tree. He jumped but soon heard a bird singing and realised that it was a lark who had upset him.

'Should I ask Rahti's permission to take her cycle away or should

27

I not?' he mumbled to himself in order to avoid being jumpy and to fill the vacancy in his mind, which was in danger of being occupied by instinctive dreads. But he did not resolve the question, though he went on repeating it like a wordless incantation.

Fatah, who was on guard at the door of the courtyard, again ran shouting loudly: 'Save me. Save me!'

Maqbool ran after him, caught him and shook him, saying: 'Hatto, it is me, Maqbool!'

Fatah looked at Maqbool terror-stricken, but remained silent as though mesmerised.

Maqbool left him and got to the verandah. He found the ladies bicycle standing by the door, and he just announced:

'Rahti Khala, I am taking your bicycle away!' And he rode away without waiting for an answer.

Afterwards, he felt guilty that she might need it to go to the town to fetch something for Salaama. But knowing that the town was in the grip of those who had sacked the convent, he surmised that the machine was useless to her.

Once he was astride the bicycle, he seemed to feel more free. The distance from the convent to his own lane was about a mile by the detour on the outskirt of the town, half of it through the fairly safe grove of chenar trees and the other half across the footpath where the town houses ended in swamps, pools and puddles.

A lean dog yelped away from above the debris of fallen leaves in the grove, and, again, he was startled out of his wits. But the dog seemed more frightened of him as he ran shrieking away.

Further up, a flock of ducks whirred over the chenar trees. He looked up and saw that their wings were touched with the silver of the risen sun above the giant hills. An involuntary sigh escaped his lips at the realisation of the total misery into which this land of the poet's dreams and visions had been suddenly plunged by the invasion. And he began to hum the words of the old Kashmiri poet Majoor:

'O Kashmir, my beloved motherland,
When the morning of a new life
Dawns upon the world
Its first ray will kiss your own
High and beautiful forehead!'

At the end of the grave, on a small platform by the deserted tomb of a Pir, he saw half a dozen men, raiders by the look of them, kneeling in the attitude of Sajdah prayer, their eyes closed, their faces turned towards the West.

Would they break off from their prayers to challenge him?

His heart beat fast. His face went pale. And his eyes were full of mist.

All the six men got up with hands folded before them and did not look this side or that, but persevered in their prayers.

He was safe.

It was a miracle that none of them had been walking about or sitting down, preparing for prayer. And the irony of it struck him, as he reached past the tomb, to the cover of some fishermen's huts, that these brutal men could be devoutly praying, though only the previous night, perhaps they had been looting and murdering. Or this bunch might be the more decent among the invaders!...Or perhaps they were just simple, fanatical barbarians, who really believed in the holy war, in which,they had been told, they were engaged here, and their prayers were merely automatic gestures, repeated without any understanding of the meaning of the Arabic words. This question of whether there was a God or not, had always oppressed him. The death of innocents had proved that there was no God, except that Allah might just now be looking after him.

The benefit of doubt could be given to God, because there were three small fishing boats tied to pegs by the riverside, and the stream was not too wide, as also utter silence prevailed on the road.

The chance of a safe passage by the river started a nausea in his stomach. The bile came into his mouth.

Strange that when a man resolved to do something, the remnants of weakness hidden in the body reacted against him.

He spat out the bile.

Then quickly he put the bicycle into the smallest of the boats, going back to untie the rope from the wooden peg.

'The oars! The oars! Where were the oars?'

His heart sank when he knew that the fishermen seldom left their oars behind.

Grimly, he accepted the fact that he would have to drift down, steering the boat with his hand, and hope that, before the end of the mile where the town began, he would have crossed the hundred yards or so to the other side.

The current was swift and panic seized him.

Desperately, he lowered the cycle into the river at the end of the boat and began to steer with its hulk. The wheels were like sieves, but the middle part seemed to work, tilting the boat ever so slightly in the opposite direction.

Seeing the distance that separated him from the objective, he nearly wanted to pray. But the current was strong and gave no promise that his indifferent oar would succeed. So no gratitude was due to anyone.

Resourcefully, he lowered his torso and joined his arm to the chain wheel.

This was more effective. He persisted.

The swift current helped him, though the boat was only three fourths of the way by the time it had floated down nearly half a mile.

There was nothing to do, but to lie down, keep the nearly frozen arm adjusted to the broadest part of the bicycle and steer clear of the

30

danger.

Time seemed to become endless.

And yet a furlong before the footbridge his boat entered a small swampy rivulet which gave him cover. Also, there was a garbage heap across which he could climb out with his bicycle.

As he crossed the garbage heap the bile rose in his mouth again, this time with the stink of the refuse as well as the tension inside him.

He contemplated the slithery slopes of the mound of rubbish with a deliberate will to accept them. Perhaps, it is necessary, as Islam taught, to go through the sewer before one could come clean. And he was doing so literally now. That would be the inner core of the poem, if he lived to write one. Also he must not forget even a single aspect of the squalor, now, as he had always done in his attraction towards love poetry. Like Jigar he had wanted to escape from asafoetida of his home town, the decay and the hopelessness. Perhaps, all the arid souls around him, his poor father, his mother, would appreciate the high pitch of his words now after what they had seen. And they would awaken rather than accept their fates.

He was through to the unpaved road.

He quickly got astride the bicycle.

Just at this moment, he seemed to himself most lucid, as though his awareness had become, through the dangers that faced him, an all enveloping, comprehensive intelligence, percolating to his senses and putting them on a plane where he had a permanent and tender understanding of human cowardice.

The sun beat faster and faster behind his back, though the draught which blew from the murky little lanes was chilling.

The prolonged stretch of a big puddle, under the shadow of the wooden houses, just before his lane, forced him to alight from his cycle.

As he free-wheeled the machine, he saw Juma, Qadri and Saleem Bux, the three brothers who worked in Muratib's carpet factory, looking at him from the cavernous room which they occupied on the ground floor by the vegetable field of Ala Din, the eccentric gardener. Before he could warn them, they shouted their greetings with the warm enthusiasm of complete innocence.

'Ah Maqbool!...Where have you been? They are everywhere... Have they also got to Srinagar?...'

Maqbool shushed them and nearly slipped over the edges of mud which he was negotiating. But it was of no avail. The fear crazed females of the household came out, and began to smile and shout greetings:

'Salaam elekum!'

'Wa elekum salaam!' Maqbool answered softly and raised his hand to silence them.

'They looted the carpet factory, Maqbool. And then set it on fire!' the old mother of Juma, Qadri and Saleem Bux shouted. 'Sons of Eblis!...They even came here! But I gave them a bit of my mind and they went away!...'

'Mother,' he said coming up to the platform on which they all stood. 'We have to be patient...'

'Patience!' the old woman shrieked. 'They have burnt the factory from which came our living, and you ask us to be patient!...What has happened to you all?...'

'Mother!...Mother!...' her sons cautioned her.

'You are all cowards!' the old woman shouted with such force that the hens on the garbage by her doorsteps fluttered away.

'I will go and see Muratib Ali,' said Maqbool. 'Do you think he will be at home?'

'What can he do? Nothing!' the old woman said cynically. 'He just sat at home and allowed the factory to be looted!'

32

'Mother, don't make such a noise!' Juma said again. 'The Pakistanis wanted carpets for their homes!...'

'Fool, don't you see,' the old woman said cocking her left eye, 'that my voice will keep those beasts away till Maqbool can get home.'

Maqbool's face puckered into a smile as he walked away towards Muratib Ali's big house in the main street, at the end of the lane.

There was the old unruly drumming under his chest as Maqbool reached the sitting room of Syed Muratib Ali's house. The young factory owner was smoking the hookah as he sat in an English armchair, and he looked up at Maqbool with a quizzical expression, which was part pleasure, part horror. For a moment neither of them said anything, as the visitor was breathless, while the host was dazed at the sudden arrival of this nationalist partisan. Then Muratib Ali said:

'Why have you come back?—To put your head in the noose?'

Maqbool did not answer, but sat down on a wicker chair opposite him, still out of breath.

'Things are terrible! You must fly from here!'

'I saw a sentry at the head of the lane. So I had to slip past him, pretending to be on business. And then I ran upstairs...'

'You seem to bear your life on the palm of your hands with a strange bravado!' Muratib said. 'Suppose the sentry had challenged you!'

'One has to take chances,' said Maqbool laconically.

'But do you realise, Maqbool brother!' Muratib began in a mildly admonishing tone. 'Do you know?...'

'Our leaders have sent me,' Maqbool cut in, knowing that only the magic word 'leaders' would justify his behaviour here in the eyes

33

of Muratib, as it had done to Mahmdoo, though there was the danger that his friend might suspect some vanity in his association of the exalted with his mission. He realised that he did feel vain from the connection, but it would be stupid if Muratib found this in him.

'The situation has gone beyond our leaders,' said Muratib. And then he began to puff at the hookah with a bored expression which was a cover for the terror which pervaded him. And as he looked away, his face seemed to betoken the attitude that Maqbool was not welcome.

There was a silence between them during which the gurgling of the hubble-bubble assumed exaggerated proportion.

Unable to bear the suspense, Muratib said:

'If I were you, Maqbool, I should make myself scarce.'

'But I am not you,' Maqbool said with a trace of arrogance in his voice which he tried to convert into humility. 'I am under orders... Besides, I feel that, on principle, we must struggle...If we believe in freedom from these "Muslim Brethren" as we believed in freedom from the British and their friends...'

He felt priggish after he had said this, especially as he fancied there was an embarrassed smile on the mouth of Muratib Ali. So he hung his head down in order to beckon that feeling of humility to come to him through which his attitude could become clear to his friend, without explanation, and through which he could summon the necessary strength to move him.

'Principles!' Muratib minced the words between his front teeth. 'Where are the arms to back the principles?'

Maqbool realised that if there had been the armed strength to give the invaders a fight, Muratib might have appreciated the principles.

'The Indian army...' he said, in a voice which betrayed a degree of wishfulfilment.

Muratib merely waved his head, pushed the hookah aside, flushed red and then said:

34

'Your friends accepted the partition of India! They betrayed their principles! Where is their secular state now?... And they allowed those who believed in divide and rule to dominate the country!...Now, it may be too late even if they do come to our help—'

'But our coreligionists in Pakistan have sold out completely,' said Maqbool with a suppressed anger in his voice. 'And you know it!...Do you think these Pakistanis would have come here without the knowledge of the British Commander-in-Chief of the Pakistan army?'

'Too bad,' said Muratib in a doleful tone. 'You have probably heard that they looted my factory...' And he rubbed his hands on the warm Kashmiri dressing gown he was wearing.

Maqbool was sorry for Muratib, though the whining acceptance by his friend irritated him. For he guessed that Muratib had enough money left over in his Srinagar Bank, as well as in Lahore and Delhi, where he exported his carpets and shawls, never really to be in need.

'I met Juma and his brothers,' he said to transfer his sympathy to those who deserved it more. 'Their mother does not seem to be frightened of the killers. She was abusing them roundly as I passed by their house. The old woman has spirit...'

'There you go—with your half baked ideas,' said Muratib resentful of Maqbool's lack of sympathy for him and because he could immediately sense an indirect comment on his weakness in Maqbool's praise for Juma's mother.

Maqbool did not say anything, but he felt calm because Muratib's lack of will confirmed his own line of action. At least that much was certain—his love for others, whatever else he knew or did not know. Meanwhile Muratib could live in his separate tragic cycle of cynicism. Surprisingly enough the factory owner's awe-inspiring fatalism was combined with an acute sense of factuality, from the stark statements he had made about politics.

He looked up at the thick set, wellfed frame of his friend, with the shy brown eyes and the curly hair.

'My mother and wife have been weeping since yesterday,'

Muratib said furtively turning his eyes away from Maqbool. 'And I owe a responsibility to them, brother, which I must put before everything else—'

Maqbool realised from these words, what Mahmdoo had taught him by now to sense, that everyone was involved in his vicious circles.

'I too have a mother, a sister, and a father,' he answered. But again, after he had said these words, he regretted that he had been so gauche and childish, putting his own ego, moth-eaten by fears, against his friend's separateness.

'And I don't suppose you have seen them!' taunted Muratib. 'You went away without telling them where you were going, and they have been hysterical with worry, thinking you were dead!...'

For a moment, Maqbool felt ashamed to acknowledge the truth of this charge. But he had told his sister where he was going and therein lay his confidence. Muratib was exaggerating. At least Noor could not have been hysterical. She was a good girl and believed in him. She might not have told his mother and father where he had gone, but surely she had reassured them that he was not dead...And they should have understood. For often he had gone out for days into the villages on political work, and, by now, they had surely begun to accept the fact that he was a dedicated person. Somehow, he felt he could not work up that kind of emotion about his family which Muratib felt. And, for good or ill, that was so.

'I told Noor that I was going to Srinagar,' he said tamely. Then after a pause he said, 'One has to do certain things in which one cannot take one's blood relations along...'

'Acha, Hatto, you are a hero!' said Muratib impatiently.

The undercurrent of mockery in Muratib's voice annoyed Maqbool. But he accepted it, and the accompanying hostility, as the well deserved punishment for daring to ask suddenly from a man, whose soul was in pawn to money and privilege and family ties, to abandon all this for what seemed just now to be no more than a slogan or a shibboleth. He sat there with head hung down.

'To tell you the truth,' continued Muratib, but did not finish.

Maqbool understood from Muratib's face that his presence was not welcome.

'I will go,' he said getting up from the chair abruptly.

But now Muratib jumped up shouting 'no' and went and embraced him and said, with tears in his eyes:

'Maqbool, forgive me, I am a coward! I really do not want you to go...'

'There is no talk,' consoled Maqbool. And with that detached warmth with which the ceremonial embrace between men is conducted, he pressed his torso against Muratib's chest. The passion which he could not work up in himself for his friend had yielded to personal affection.

And now those springs of tenderness were also released in Muratib, which had so far remained hidden in him:

'I know there will be no peace in our land until we have fought them, Maqbool!' the factory owner said, 'I feel sad in my heart...But we are deserted. Everyone seems to have been cowed down. And I have become a coward!...'

'No, no, brother,' interrupted Maqbool separating from his friend. 'We are all liable to fear. Only, if we allow fear to grip our souls, we become cowardly. And each one of us is capable of this, in a situation like the one we are in...'

'Perhaps it is so, but I am not a poet and do not know all the things,' said Muratib sitting down on the edge of his chair, his face covered with his hands. 'But the coterie of friends, that we were, are now separated...You will not accept...I am frightened...And Ghulam is under the thumb of his father. And the only person who could have advised him, your clever friend, lawyer Ahmed Shah, in whom you believed, even against my advice, has gone over...' Saying this he passed his right hand over his forehead and face, as though to cast off the oppression from his visage.

'I was a fool about Ahmed Shah,' agreed Maqbool, realising that he had, indeed, been always too impressed by Ahmed Shah's brilliant talk to apprehend his real temperament.

'I remember well,' said Muratib, 'that when you made him President of the National Conference branch of Baramula, I told you that he was an opportunist, who would use the movement only for his own ends. He needed that prestige to work up his practice...'

'He had a fairly good practice before,' Maqbool put in as a corrective. But he realised that he himself had never been wise and tended to take people at their word rather than as human beings pulled by different desires and ambitions. 'Though I confess,' he added, 'that you did warn me and you have been proved right...I was not shrewd enough to anticipate his reactions to the changed situation...But Ghulam is, I know, a good man at heart, however he may be swayed...'

'He is weak,' said Muratib. 'Even weaker than me. He cannot cut the connection with his father, as I cannot deny my mother and my wife.'

'I will try to talk to Ghulam,' said Maqbool.

Muratib laughed a little and shrugged his shoulders. And Maqbool became aware that the vague sense of hostility, fear and indifference towards him and the things he represented, were creeping back into his friend's soul. Most people here would feel that he was valueless. And he thought, nostalgically, of the fighting spirit built up by the friends in Srinagar, the enthusiasm and the doggedness which he had never seen among the people of Kashmir before. How was he to communicate that to his brethren in the occupied town of Baramula?

'Talk is cheap, brother,' said Muratib. 'But what plan have you brought with you? What are we to do?'

'I know you have always despised words,' Maqbool protested. 'I have only a voice. And it is all we can do to talk to each other. To strengthen our morale. To resist in our minds the idea of occupation by the "Muslim brethren". To sabotage their plans. And to survive until help comes from Srinagar...'

Muratib looked up at Maqbool and, after all, allowed some real warmth to come into him for the earnestness of his friend. He was even stirred by a wave of admiration.

'If a little money can help,' he said, 'you can have it! Frustrate their plans and try to survive until help comes from Jawaharlal.'

Maqbool sensed the measure of Muratib's support and accepted the fact without even a mental protest. Perhaps it was good enough that, in spite of the loss of his factory, Muratib was still offering money. That material support was not to be despised. And though there were too many gaps in Muratib's understanding of the struggle and his sympathies, it seemed that he would, nevertheless, not go against what he, Maqbool, knew was worth struggling for.

'May I go to Ghulam's house?' Maqbool asked Muratib.

'It is dangerous,' said Muratib. 'Go home to your people. I will try and send a message to Ghulam to come and see you.'

'Then he would be in danger,' said Maqbool.

'Here is some money,' Muratib said handing him a wad of notes. Maqbool thrust the notes into his pocket and shook hands with Muratib a little shyly, and, without looking at him, walked away.

'God be with you!' said Muratib contemplating the youthful figure of the poet disappearing into the darkness of the hall on top of the stairs.

Maqbool had to affect the casual effrontery of an inmate of the big house as he came into the lane, free-wheeling the bicycle, so that he could will himself into the necessary pose of ordinary behaviour before he should pass by the Pakistan sentry on his way to the house of Ghulam Jilani in the middle of the main bazar.

This made him feel as though he was striking a semi-heroic pose and he relaxed from the dramatic attitude as he actually emerged into the bazar.

The street was empty, except for a Pathan sentry and some raiders who were sitting on a bench outside the shop of the confectioner, Amira, drinking their morning tea.

The sentry turned to him, as though from habit, even as he held the steaming cup away from his mouth. And, for one instant Maqbool's heart congealed, bringing an involuntary tremor of weakness in his legs. Then, with an almost physical exertion of his will, he converted his dazed apprehension into a smile and, with a loud bluff in his voice, called to the confectioner:

'Amira Hatto, cup of hot tea.'

'Come, come, Maqbool Sahib!' the confectioner greeted him. 'Will you have a kulcha with your tea?'

'No, you know that I don't eat first thing in the morning,' he said to establish the fact that he was a daily visitor at this shop and he hoped that the name 'Maqbool' by which Amira had addressed him, meant that he was known to him.

Amira looked at him a little quizzically, as he began to pour the tea, while Maqbool came and stood, with the saddle of the bicycle resting on his posterior, astride the bench on which the Pathans sat.

'Salt tea or sugar?' asked Amira.

Maqbool winced because such a question was sure to betray him: if he was a regular visitor. Surely Amira would know about his taste. Fortunately, Amira had asked him this in Kashmiri.

'All Kashmiris drink salt tea,' said Maqbool quickly in Punjabi to show that they were not saying anything unusual to each other in Kashmiri. 'I did not know you even made tea with sugar.'

Amira realised that he had been foolish and tried to put the situation back to normal by saying:

'Our guests here prefer tea with sugar.'

'I cannot understand, you Kashmiris drinking tea with salt!' commented the sentry in his broken accented frontier Punjabi.

'Foolish folk!' said one of the other Pathans, shaking his head with a trace of arrogance and contempt in his voice.

'They are Muslims, though,' the sentry said, 'like us. Only they have been too long with *Kafirs*.'

40

'That Hindu Maharaja is known to be very fond of white women!...' another raider put in. And he winked at his companions.

At this they all laughed and sniggered.

Maqbool too smiled, but tried to cover up his lack of enthusiasm for their talk by taking the cup of tea offered to him by the confectioner.

As he stood back, the handle of the bicycle erratically swerved and he nearly dropped the tea in his confusion.

'Put the steel horse away and sit down here,' the sentry said.

Maqbool took the advice as the easiest way out of the awkward situation.

The tea was scalding hot and he began to blow at it in the spitting-spattering manner of the Kashmiris. And he took advantage of the inclination of his head over the cup to survey the faces of the enemies with surreptitious glances. They were highly tanned, all of them, except for one who was fair-complexioned and blue eyed, with red cheeks. Their torsos bristled with cartridge belts. But their clothes exuded the odour of sour sweat, which came in waves towards his nostrils.

They too became aware of the fact that he was a literate man and somebody. So the sentry asked him as politely as he could in his accented Punjabi accent:

'Why are Kashmiris so effeminate!...You ride a woman's steel horse?...Why?...'

'I have a motor cycle,' replied Maqbool knowing that his status would go up immediately if he said this: 'But there is no petrol available...So I borrowed my sister's bicycle.'

Amira was nearly going to rebut this lie with his raised eyebrows but checked himself in time.

Maqbool hurried with his tea, thinking that the longer he stayed here the more difficult conversation might become for him.

'In this they are like us—they drink scalding hot tea!' said the red-cheeked Pathan.

'Also, they eat Nan and Kulcha!' said another.

'But they stink!' said another. 'I cannot go near the latrine, in the house where I am!... Toba! Toba!'

'To be sure! To be sure! To be sure!' the others chimed in and laughed.

'La hol billa! No talk of refuse early in the morning!' said the sentry deprecating the unholy talk.

Maqbool had been keeping up a smile as he drank tea. When he finished with some alacrity, and paid Amira, he directed a Salaam elekam, with a hearty bluff, towards the raiders. And then, with a smart sweep of his salwar, he rode off.

'One of our leaders!' blurted out the unfortunate dunce Amira.

Maqbool did not slow down to hear any more, but paddled along the length of a furlong to Ghulam Jilani's house. The stray sentries at the head of other lanes saw him pass. But they had also seen him sitting by their compatriots on the bench outside the confectioner's shop.

When he had gone half way, however, the raiders outside Amira's shop were shouting to the other sentries.

He paddled faster.

But soon a shot rang out beside him.

He did not turn to look, but raced along, aware that they had got to know of him. His legs were collapsing under him, as their shouts tingled in his brain. But his eyes were set almost as though in a reverie. The bitter taste of defeat was in his mouth. He could see Ghulam Jilani's house like a mirage before his eyes. He ground the saliva in his mouth, puffed and darted into the gulley, where the side approach to the house lay. He was in luck. The door was open. And Ibil, the old bearded servant, sat smoking the hookah on a charpoy.

'Maqbool!' the old man greeted him warmly for he had known him as Ghulam's friend since they were children.

'Not a word!' Maqbool cautioned him.

And, leaning the bicycle by a wall, he proceeded upstairs, leaving Ibil gasping for breath at the realisation of the danger in which Maqbool might be, considering that he was a firebrand.

Ghulam Jilani was pouring tea for a tall handsome stranger and

42

for lawyer Ahmed Shah, as Maqbool entered the big old Kashmir style reception room covered with carpets and cow-tailed cushions. None of the three people on the diwan got up as he entered, but all of them looked at him, Ghulam embarrassed and surprised, Ahmed Shah with a contemptuous twist of his mouth and the stranger with a blank stare.

'Come, come,' said Ghulam with an effort at cordiality, 'come and have some breakfast.'

He deliberately avoided welcoming him by name. And Maqbool understood that his friend was seeking to shield him from the stranger, who was presumably one of the officials of the invading army.

'Khurshid Sahib,' began Ahmed Shah in a slightly bantering tone. 'This is Muhammad Maqbool Sherwani!...'

The stranger moved his head briefly, but remained immobile with a conceited smirk on his lips.

Maqbool sensed that Khurshid Anwar knew him to be one of the men of the Kashmir national movement.

There was no retreat from this situation, because to go downstairs into the street was to court death at the hands of the tribesmen, who had got to know his identity from the confectioner; while, if this man was, indeed, Khurshid Anwar, he, Maqbool, had walked straight into the lion's mouth. However he walked politely up to sit by the edge of the white cloth on which breakfast was laid out.

Ghulam Jilani kept his face bent, probably because he did not want to betray any emotion, but his fair-complexioned round visage flushed a vivid red and betrayed his confusion. And he went on pouring the tea in order to keep his eyes averted from the guests. After he had filled the cup, he put in the milk and two spoonfuls of sugar, and he offered tea to Maqbool.

Maqbool took it and, affecting a naturalness which he did not feel, said:

'I am sorry to disturb you so early in the morning—without a warning!'

'When have you ever announced your arrival?' said Ahmed Shah challengingly. 'You workers of the National Conference are like Communists—always very earnest and very busy.'

Maqbool's first impulse was to return the compliment by re-minding him that he himself had once been a President of the Baramula branch of the National Conference; that, in fact, he had manoeuvred to be elected to this position, but he felt that would be completely unworthy of him. So he kept silent.

Ghulam Jilani's face was nearly beetroot now.

For a moment there was a secret exertion of wills and a blind war of impulses in all the four men. While Ahmed Shah ate chunks of bread and butter, even as he picked up a white fried egg on his fork so precariously poised that Ghulam Jilani and Maqbool Sherwani both nervously stared at his hands, praying that he would perform the miracle and catch it up in his mouth, without dropping it. He did so and they relaxed.

But Ahmed Shah, who had seen them watch his performance, was unnerved enough at the deep roots of his sense of inferiority and he broke the silence with a violent attack on Maqbool.

'You are a strange person! Never letting us know where you go!...Why were you not here to welcome our friends? They will never forgive your defection to the camp of Hindu Maharaja...I suppose you have come back now that you know the people of Srinagar are on our side and are ready to welcome—'

'There is no question of forgiveness, as there had been no defection,' Maqbool cut in. 'And the people of Srinagar are not ready to welcome the raiders...'

'We shall soon decide whom they will welcome,' said Khurshid Anwar, provoked by what he considered to be Maqbool's effrontery. 'Our army has outflanked Srinagar, from Gandarbal, and we shall soon make a frontal attack!'

The strong Punjabi accent of his Hindustani speech annoyed Maqbool on aesthetic grounds, even as Khurshid Anwar's whole western style aggressive personality roused a blind yearning in him

44

to go away from the man's presence. Anwar's English clothes seemed to revive the humiliation at the hands of the white sahib tourists in Kashmir. But he brought all the self control he possibly could to bear on his being, though he could not help answering back.

'Why, then, haven't you made the frontal attack?...Are you frightened of the Indian army coming to our rescue?...'

'Oh no!...no, no!' Khurshid Anwar said with a blustering half laugh. 'Let my boys secure the base in Baramula and compensate themselves for their trouble in coming all the way from Peshawar and Abbotabad—then we shall move forward. There are still riches hidden in the houses of Kashmiri Pandits, even if they have taken the Panditanis away!...'

At this Ghulam Jilani blushed visibly. And even Ahmed Shah was ashamed enough to want to cover up the obscene strategy with brave talk.

'Khurshid Sahib is joking, to be sure,' he began. 'But this expedition has been planned by one of the bravest officers of Pakistan army!...Mr. Jinnah himself is in Lahore, waiting for good news of our accession to Pakistan. And in Mirpur and Poonch, the Azad Kashmir movement has already set up its own government under Sardar Muhammad Ibrahim...Gilgit has also fallen...Now if only we had sense, we would have voluntarily offered to unite with Pakistan rather than hitch our wagon to the Maharaja's fading star— and Hindu India...'

'There is nothing but contempt in our minds. Maharaja Hari Singh has fled with his bag and baggage to Jammu—'

'Cowards can't stand and fight,' Khurshid Anwar said boredly.

'Drink up your tea, Khurshid Sahib,' said the weak Ghulam Jilani, thinking that the only way out of this discussion was to concentrate on breakfast and hope for a miraculous termination of the controversy.

'Don't be so solemn always!' said Ahmed Shah trying to humour

Maqbool in case he should flare up against Khurshid Anwar's effrontery.

But Maqbool had recognised himself in his own will and was now bent on courting disaster since it had come to him.

'How can you sit by, and see your home town sacked—and looted!...What have we come to?...'

'Why, whose house has been looted?' Ahmed Shah asked. 'Yours?...Have you been home and seen?...Not mine, nor Jilani Sahib's!...'

'Our friend, Muratib has lost his factory,' said Maqbool.

'Only because he was a fool and too mean to give some presents of carpets to our guests!'

'Strange talk!' Maqbool said raising his voice. 'Friendship seems to mean nothing to you!'

'Don't bark!' challenged Ahmed Shah getting up and pathetically seeking to dominate Maqbool with his small five-foot frame.

Ghulam Jilani jumped up and dragged him down with the words:

'Ahmed Shah—Maqbool Sahib differs from you! That is all! Try and convert him! You are a lawyer!...'

'In order to destroy anarchy,' thundered Ahmed Shah pale in the face, 'we will also resort to anarchy and violence. I believe in reasoning with intelligent men, not with fools!...I want union with Pakistan...I believe in a Central Muslim state, which will be a counter to Communism in the north, and to the Bania Hindu Raj in the South...And we can connect up with our brethren in the Middle East and revive the glory of ancient Islamic democracy in a world ridden with unbelief!...The poet Iqbal himself preached this. How should this village idiot, pretending to be a poet, know the intricacies of our design, the concept of Muslim Federation!...I know more about this than all of you...'

The last words were so gauche that both Ghulam Jilani and Khurshid Anwar turned their faces away from him.

'You do not believe in your own words,' Maqbool thrust the rapier home. 'How can anyone believe in your words?...'

'I shall murder you!' Ahmed Shah raged and got up again.

This time it was not Ghulam Jilani but Khurshid Anwar who pulled him back: and the latter did not have to use his obvious physical strength, but only a few words:

'You leave that to me, Ahmed Shah!...Just sit down and don't be so jumpy. Let me settle with our friend...'

Ahmed Shah sat down docilely enough.

'Ahmed Shah Abdali's logic!' mocked Maqbool comparing him to the infamous Afghan invader of a century ago.

'Stop mocking at him!' bullied Khurshid Anwar. 'You are not much of a hero either! Running away from home. Then sneaking back to spy and curry favour with your rich friends—'

'I have poor friends also,' cut in Maqbool, though he realised the folly of having come here. 'The people will not easily reconcile themselves to burning and loot.'

'Stop this tain tain and listen to me,' shouted Khurshid with a vulgar tone in his voice, 'I am a straightforward Punjabi and not given to argument. And don't sell me any of your bluff about the people. Islam is a brotherhood in which there are no distinctions, such as the Hindus make—'

'All one happy family in Pakistan!' interrupted Maqbool. 'Mr. Jinnah and the refugees and all!—'

'I have asked you not to interrupt me,' shouted Khurshid Anwar.

'You are not God!' challenged Maqbool desperate like an animal at bay and boiling with a violent inner fury.

'No, but listen—I give you a choice: You can have as honourable a place in the brotherhood of Islam as Ghulam Jilani and Ahmed Shah have. Or you will be handed over to our forces to meet the justice due to spies and traitors!'

'I am neither spy nor traitor!...I put Kashmir above everything. I have some principles. And you—'

47

'It is no use talking to him,' intervened Ahmed Shah. 'A petty, conceited creature. He has not the vision to see anything beyond Baramula. He has never even been to Lahore! And he will not be grateful if you show him mercy. He will want to stab you in the back...A low cur!...'

This abuse cut into the generous spirit of Ghulam Jilani who objected:

'Ahmed Shah Sahib, please do not use such language. Maqbool has been our friend. And as he says, it is a question of his principles. He has chosen his side, as you have chosen yours—'

'Where do you stand, Mr. Jilani?' asked Khurshid Anwar, unnerved by what seemed like the defection of his host. 'Your father has already decided!'

'To be sure, I am with my father,' said Ghulam Jilani sheepishly. 'But I believe in friendship. I think you can talk to Maqbool and make him see reason. And once he sees it and promises to be with you, he will keep his word—that I can assure you!'

Having no tact, Khurshid Anwar was persuaded by the superior tact of the landlord's son, seasoned in the courtesies of the court. He knew that the approach suggested by Ghulam Jilani would have been better than the argumentation of Ahmed Shah. He himself had tried to keep calm, but the impetuosity of the lawyer had thrust him into a debate.

'You know your friend better,' conceded Khurshid. 'But you realise that we are living in a time of decision. We cannot just leave things vague. We have to choose!'

'Maqbool is my guest, as you are,' Ghulam Jilani urged. 'And I would not like to misuse the fact of his visit here to impose a decision on him. Nor to ask him to choose immediately. He need not commit himself. He can think things over and see reason—'

'I could only see reason in a reasonable world,' Maqbool said. 'But after this sudden invasion and the murders—'

'This is a war of liberation!' protested Ahmed Shah. 'A war! An historic event! We are passing through times which will decide our destiny forever. And everyone has to choose now!...'

'I will certainly not be bullied by you,' interrupted Maqbool. 'I don't believe in this historic event—we were living peacefully enough and struggling against wrongs...And then these people came, with guns pointed at us, demanding accession by force—'

'I shall have you arrested, if you don't hold your tongue!' shouted Khurshid Anwar.

The ring of truth in Maqbool's voice seemed to threaten the outer edge of Khurshid Anwar's complacency. So he reacted before his words could penetrate any further into the areas of doubt. For he had his own reasons for being in on this affray, and these were only thinly garbed in the veneer of patriotism.

'Khurshid Sahib, you cannot do anything to my guest,' protested Jilani, beckoning courage from his fat body and reddening in the attempt to do so.

'Ghulam Jilani,' Khurshid answered disclosing the crudeness of his bandit's soul. 'I was going to let you off with the payment of only one lakh as conscience money. It may now become two lakhs—'

'I don't mind the money,' said Ghulam Jilani, 'But you will allow Maqbool to leave.'

'What are you doing and saying?...' protested Ahmed Shah turning to Ghulam Jilani. 'Don't you see?...'

'I am saying or doing nothing which is not according to the traditions of Islam,' said Jilani. 'A guest is sacred to me...'

Maqbool touched Ghulam Jilani's arm tenderly. At this Ghulam got up, with a strange dignity in his rolly polly frame, shook his friend's hand and took him into his arms.

Khurshid looked at this phenomena and was strangely moved.

Maqbool dislocated himself from Ghulam's embrace, and, without heeding Ahmed Shah, walked away towards the door.

'May God be with you!' Ghulam mumbled as Maqbool went down the stairs.

'Your cycle,' called Ghulam Jilani.

49

'It is too dangerous to ride it,' said Maqbool. 'I shall leave it with Ibil downstairs. Send it to the convent to my aunt Rahti. I will have to go through the byelanes and not on the highway...' And he added bitterly: 'I shall leave the main roads for Ahmed Shah when he goes on the victory parade...'

As Maqbool descended the stairs, old Ibil greeted him with a solemn face, which was made more profound by the fingers that he had put on his lips, indicating not to whisper. And he led the young man towards the inner hallway leading to the zenana.

'The Pakistanis are outside, asking for you,' Ibil said.

Maqbool felt very foolish standing there like that with the bicycle under his right arm. Ibil had realised his predicament and, with the tact of the useful uncle, he took the machine from him and put it in the alcove where the fuel wood was stored. Then he came stood towering over Maqbool and said with a dry wit peculiar to him:

'It is better for a man to ride the machine than for a machine to ride the man.'

Maqbool sensed that old Ibil, having lived through the same experiences as everyone else in Baramula, had dropped the opiate insouciance of the servant of the feudal household and seemed to cherish the same simple desire for action and the same anxieties. He was not surprised, therefore, when the man suggested:

'We have to evolve a stratagem by which we can contrive to get you out of this place to some safe hideout... And it has occurred to me that the only way to get you out of here is to lend you the Begum's burqah, also a female attendant. Then the Pathans will not dare to look your way...They still have some respect for the Begum of the landlord...'

Before such logic Maqbool could only bow respectfully, though he tried to make sure.

'But the Begum Sahiba—?'

'I have already told the Begum Sahib you are upstairs. And she has expressed the wish to see you. So you come with me. I shall get my wife, Habiba, to escort you by way of the sub-lane to the main bazar to your house.'

Maqbool watched the old man's wizened face and saw the warmth which transfused it. As he looked steadily, tears came into his own eyes. And, before they became obvious, he began to walk towards the zenana as Ibil followed.

'Begum Sahib may be in her bath,' said Ibil coming forward. 'I shall go ahead of you.' And immediately, he called out: 'Habiba— Maqbool Sahib is here. Will the Begum Sahiba receive him?'

There was a fluttering of forms and confused whispers, so that both Maqbool and Ibil halted deliberately to wait and give the females time for cover. At length Habiba answered:

'Ao. I am just putting henna on Begum Sahiba's head!'

Maqbool stepped forward, with his head bent. But he was able to take in the situation. Begum Mehtab Jilani was seated on her diwan, while Habiba was plastering the red dye on her hair.

Maqbool, son, there is no purdah from you,' the Begum said. 'But what a time you have chosen to arrive!'

'I am unlucky,' Maqbool said realising that, apart from her hospitality, she too, like her son, wished he had not embarrassed her household with his awkward presence.

'Come and sit down by me,' the Begum said.

Maqbool obeyed as docilely as he had always done as a child.

'Habiba,' Ibil beckoned to his wife.

The maid looked at the Begum and the mistress nodded her head.

'Life is cruel,' the Begum began philosophically. 'As a woman I have known this truth. We have to accept, because in the eyes of Allah, we deserve the punishment. The only way, son, in which this cruelty can be offset is by obedience to destiny. What is written in one's fate will be...I was born a woman. So it was no use my protesting against fate. I had to accept, but acceptance brought contentment. I must admit that, when I came as a young woman, to the house of Sardar Jilani, I was afraid. I decided to obey him. I could not do certain things, and yet everything was really in my hands. He ruled me, but I ruled the household...Now these new rulers demand obedience. But, perhaps, if we accept their rule, we will be free to do what we like in our own households...Only Allah the just knows everything...'

'If I may say so, respectfully,' said Maqbool, 'when death is opposed to life, then life must oppose death...I know there will be much bloodshed, and ruin in this way, but the urge for freedom cannot be suppressed...'

'I know that you are as determined as all the young are,' Begum Mehtab conceded. 'And I always pointed you to my son as an example of sacrifice. But you will understand that my husband and I, and our son, have bigger responsibilities than most people.'

'I know—,' said Maqbool bitterly.

'Son,' she said briefly. 'We have to take refuge in our love for our family—and in our belief in God...'

There was silence between them.

'I know your opinion, son,' the Begum continued. 'But we have treated all our tenants as our children. Only, they are people who cannot rule themselves. They need a gentle, wise father. And Sardar Sahib has always been that at heart, however harsh he may seem at times—'

The words jarred on Maqbool's ears, because in his conscious-ness, poverty, and even the abject acceptance of that poverty by the peasantry, had become the root of all evil in Kashmir. All the hierarchy of the feudal order, from the Maharaja downwards, through his courtiers and landlords, represented a chain of humiliations, which had only to be seen and lived through to be believed. Of course, in the sequestered shades of the zenana of the landlord's house, the whole array seemed a permanent god-given order, which had to be accepted and obeyed.

'Mother,' he said with a trace of impatience in his voice. 'We can never decide this argument. Some day, perhaps you will realise that

I didn't lead your son astray as you always thought I did...But he and I have been like brothers. And, even now, at the risk of the displeasure of Khurshid Anwar, he has protected me from the invaders. You have always been to me like a mother...I want to go from your presence, as a good son and not a quarrelsome Shaitan boy...'

Begum Mehtab put her left hand on his head and said:

'But you better stay here now. Where can you go at this time, with them on all sides?'

'Begum Sahiba,' said Ibil coming forward. 'I have a plan if you will permit it. Maqbool Sahib will go in your burqah and Habiba will go with him, from the door in the small lane where there are no enemies...'

'Ibil!' said the Begum imperiously. 'Do not call them enemies. It is not seemly. But perhaps Maqbool's only way home is the way you suggest...You better ask Abdul, to yoke the horse to the tonga, and escort them yourself...To be sure, this is the best—'

She did not finish her sentence. But her heavy jaw fell with the painful pull between her humanity and the instinct for the preservation of her family.

Maqbool bowed very low to her as he rose and followed Ibil.

'I will go into the inner room,' the Begum said. 'Habiba, come back quickly. I shall be anxious about you...' And she went into the inner sanctums of the zenana.

Seated beside Habiba, huddled like a ghost in the burqah with the jallied aperture, before his eyes in the hood of the veil, disclosing nothing but the blue curtain at the back of the tonga to guard female decorum against the intrusion of stranger's stares, Maqbool went through the queerest experience of all his life. That he, Maqbool Sherwani, should go in a woman's veil seemed humiliating and foolishly histrionic. And yet it was an old stratagem of feudal households. But wouldn't the Pakistanis be reckless enough to look in to make sure.

The carriage had jog-trotted quite fifty yards without anything happening.

53

Perhaps, he felt, that the sentries outside the house of Sardar Muhammad Jilani had seen the tonga issue from the exalted one's residence and given the password to the other sentries. Still Ibil was playing with his own life, and that of his wife's in escorting him. For, if the raiders had suspected that he, Maqbool Sherwani, had probably gone into the Jilani household (since they had come knocking on the door), then the very sight of the landlord's servant would make them suspicious.

The rhythmic jolting of the horse carriage unnerved him, and he sweated inside the veil and quivered. The uneven ruts in the road shook him. And he found his mind emptying into vacancy of suspense.

'Who is there?' suddenly a Pathan sentry challenged.

'From the household of Sardar Jilani,' answered Ibil.

Soon there was the clattering of hobnailed shoes and muffled voices.

The impulse to live hovered on the fearful threat of being found out. But Maqbool looked before him without stirring. Suddenly, the purdah at the back of the tonga was lifted by two soldiers.

'Who?' one of the Pathans barked.

'Zenana,' said Habiba.

For a while, the soldiers who had not spoken, lingered and stared hard at the forms.

'Why do you annoy even females?' Ibil said aggressively. 'Among Muslims this is not done.'

The soldier dropped the curtain.

'Go ahead,' Ibil said to the coachman.

Maqbool had held his breath. The grip of his mouth was tight in spite of him and his eyes had closed. The miracle had happened again. Rescued from the very jaws of death! Would his luck hold out? he wondered. Instinctively, he found himself with the word Allah at the back of his head in thankfulness...And he reflected how strange it was that those who were, on principle, the life opposers, the family of the landlord, should have saved him at the risk of courting the

54

displeasure of their newfound friends.

The carriage advanced slowly. But in order to keep the occupants at the back informed of where they were, Ibil went on directing the coachman:

'There,' he said, 'stop by the shop of the confectioner...And wait here, till I return!...'

And, in a moment, the tonga came to a standstill.

'Please alight and I will escort you,' Ibil announced to the occupants.

Maqbool allowed Habiba to get down first. Then he got down. Ibil came near him and whispered,

'The road is clear.'

And he led the way into the gulley.

Awkward and halting, in spite of his best efforts, Maqbool advanced with an affected slouching gait behind Ibil, his heart beating involuntarily.

As they got to the middle of the lane, Ibil said in an almost audible speech:

'The sentries of this lane had taken the confectioner with them to identify someone they suspect...'

Habiba shushed him from behind the lifted headpiece of her burqah. And she led the train up to the door of Maqbool's house. And she even took the initiative in striking the suspended latch of the door to summon the household from above. Fortunately, out of the fear of the raiders, the lane was empty, except for prying eyes, who only saw the females of Sardar Jilani's house enter with the servant, Ibil, when the door was opened by Maqbool's mother.

Habiba went to Maqbool's mother and turning her eyes to the other form in burqah, whispered:

'Maqbool.'

Maqbool's mother was dazed and stared uncomprehendingly at

the figure before her.

Maqbool seemed to have surveyed the hall through the eyepiece of the burqah, and, finding the place empty, he took off the veil.

His mother put her arms around him and clung to him weeping.

'Mother, mother,' he called to her to silence her.

'I thought you were dead, Maqbool...' she sobbed. 'I thought they had killed you!'

At that instant, Maqbool's father came down, a lean, pale man with a grim and angry expression on his face.

Maqbool greeted him respectfully, almost as a stranger accosts an official: 'Salaam elekum!'

The old man answered equally formally: 'Wa elekum salaam!'

'Where is Noor?' Maqbool asked.

'She is upstairs, son,' his mother said. 'So are other people—all waiting for you. Mahmdoo of the cookshop from Pattan is here. And his son, Gula. And others...We were all worried about you. Come... And you must be hungry...'

And she led the way upstairs.

'When Gula went there at dawn to fetch you,' said Mahmdoo, the fat confectioner, 'and did not find you there, I thought that either the worst had happened and they had caught you, or that you had come home...So I asked the way here...I am happy you have come back safe...The Shaitans are everywhere...'

'But too busy looting to be very vigilant.' Maqbool put in. 'Even their leader, Khurshid Anwar, is sitting comfortably at Sardar Jilani's house to take his tribute from there, before he will do anything else. And he said his men must collect enough to compensate themselves before moving on to Srinagar—'

'One lakh is what he demands,' said Ibil, who, like all servants in a feudal household, seemed to know everything that was going on. 'Sardar Sahib had promised him fifty thousand, which is all he had in cash...'

All those assembled uttered moans of wonder and horror when they heard such big sums being mentioned. Only Maqbool protested.

56

'I would like to stop him from paying that money to this robber and crook!'

'Son, you use strong words,' Maqbool's father intervened sternly.

'Such robbery with violence calls for strong words, father!' said Maqbool.

'Now, no quarrel in our household,' the mother said. 'Chai! Noor, my child, bring the samovar over here and I will pour it.'

Maqbool's sister, Noor, an even featured girl, slightly disfigured by the pimples of youth, which she had squeezed, came over with the samovar and crouched near the company demurely, keeping her bright big eyes lowered even as she drew the headcloth over her forehead.

'You have always encouraged these children to disobedience,' said the father turning to the mother.

'Begum Jilani also believes that the highest thing in life is obedience!' Maqbool said. 'All the old people believe in obedience. We must accept and not rebel. All that happens to us is due to the fate ordained by Allah!...Say five prayers a day, keep fasts and obey—and die in the process!...'

The tone of mockery in Maqbool's voice disturbed his mother who wanted the happy family reunion to last out in the atmosphere of cordiality. So long as her chickens were safe in her coop, she felt no concern about anything outside.

The father remained silent at the rebuke, which his son had administered to him by implication. Then he burst out from the strange cavern of his fears and frustration.

'What can we do against such odds, I ask you! The salvation of our souls lies in the hands of Allah and his prophets. If we pray, perhaps Allah will hear our prayers...'

'But father,' Noor ventured, 'our brother loves the weak, she whispered. Allah does not seem to hear—'

'Silent...Noor, and don't blaspheme!' shouted the father. 'I should not have sent you to that school...!'

'Pour the tea, child,' the mother consoled Noor quickly lest the girl should burst into tears as she usually did at the least little rebuke.

'Allah has sent his apostles, the Pakistanis, our "Muslim brethren", to liberate us by depriving us of our breath!' said Maqbool with a caustic and bitter humour.

'The whole house is in revolt against me!' protested the father.

'To be sure!' Mahmdoo intervened, out of embarrassment at the family quarrel. 'But, all the same, Maqbool Sahib has been known as the friend of broken people! He is a worthy son. And you ought not to feel that he is doing anything wrong if he wants us to struggle against invaders. Our leaders have sent him to Baramula...'

This silenced the company. And Maqbool's mother used the tense calm to serve tea to everyone. Noor looked at her brother surreptitiously from the corners of her eyes, full of admiration for her brother, who had actually been talking to the great in Srinagar. Gula broke the reserve by saying naively:

'Maqbool Bhai, when shall we go to Pattan to collect the motor cycle? Will you take me to Srinagar on it?'

At this Mahmdoo laughed a brief laugh and then turned on his son:

'We are all in danger of our lives—and you, fool, think only of the motor cycle!'

'The trouble with our leaders,' began Maqbool's father, 'is that they are idealists! They love the poor, but do not realise that the poor cannot love them. All the people want is bread. And, for the rest they lie about unheeding on dung heaps! And they have no thought of Allah, but call Allah to come down.'

After a pause he continued:

'You should be in Srinagar, father,' said Maqbool, 'to see how much those whom you despise work. It is not their fault if they are unheeding. You know how the Angrezi Sarkar has ground us down and made life cheap as dust...Do you think that we do not believe in anything?...But we cannot save the soul of a person, without saving his body...We must survive...The trouble is that, in spite of their prayers, they have lost faith—they no longer seek to live by any truth in their lives...'

58

'You talk sense, son,' conceded the father looking away from Maqbool and turning to his hookah, which Noor had filled for him. And he continued: 'But then often you become mad and talk like a fanatic!'

'He is young,' apologised the mother. 'And he has reduced himself to a skeleton rushing about. He neglects to eat or drink—and he has become impatient. I would like to feed him on good food for at least a month when all this is over. Mahmdoo, you must send us some good butter from Pattan. I hear the cowherds come to your shop daily with milk and butter...'

'To be sure, mother of Maqbool,' assured Mahmdoo. 'I shall send you the good ghee as soon as this blight—'

There was the sound of knocking at the door and the faces of the whole company became pale. For a moment, the suspense hung before their wide open eyes.

Maqbool's mother looked out of the window of the sitting room and quickly turned to reassure everyone:

'Juma and his brothers!...'

'We shall beg your permission to go,' said Ibil. And he turned to Habiba, who had sat huddled up in her burqah by the shoes on the door.

Maqbool got up and saw Ibil to the door, so that he could give him some cash for his trouble. Inside the little hall, beyond the door-way, he put a ten rupee note into Ibil's hand and shook the closed fist warmly with his both hands.

Noor came up to him as he turned and said: 'Brother, take me with you to Srinagar if you go again. I can ride on the back of your motor cycle.'

Maqbool touched her cheek tenderly and said in a bantering manner:

'Noori, you will first have to get mother to allow you to wear a salwar and kurta rather than this Kashmiri gown before you can become a soldier.'

'Nothing of the kind!' warned the mother who had overheard.

'No girl of mine will become a soldier. I won't trust her out of this home, with those brutes about!'

'But mother,' assured Maqbool. 'All the young boys and girls in Srinagar have joined the military and are learning to use guns!'

'Father, I also want to go to Srinagar,' said Gula impetuously. 'Send me with Maqbool!'

'And we too want to go there!' shouted Juma. 'To Srinagar—'

'War is no joke,' Maqbool's father answered. 'There are bullets about.'

'Hatto, he has just come from Srinagar,' added Mahmdoo. 'He can't go back there without running into danger!'

'But we can't sit here, twiddling our thumbs,' said Juma.

'Especially when there is no work,' said Qadri, who was the gentler of the three brothers.

'And I for one am through with work at the factory,' said Saleem Bux. 'I want to join the army—'

'And see the world!' mocked Mahmdoo.

'It is good to hear this talk,' commented Maqbool. 'At least the young want to do something...Not like all the old ones who want to cave in...In Srinagar even the old have enlisted in the volunteer corps—'

'I suppose even the old people learn to recognise the needful when someone can make the choice for them,' said Mahmdoo.

'I understand the rich not being able to make a choice,' said Maqbool. 'I have met Muratib Ali and Ghulam Jilani. They were good friends of mine. But they are behaving like weaklings, because they are privileged. For those who are not privileged the choice is easier. We must fight against the violent destroyers of life—with violence. There is such a thing as goodness—as there is evil and lies! We are not, like the Pakistanis, exhorting people to go and slaughter! We were innocent enough. And we have been attacked. We have to fight against the...Against the tribesmen—ours is the human response of pity for those whom they have despoiled!'

The fact that he was standing as he said all this gave his words authority, though he deliberately avoided an oratorical tone of speech. For he had a horror of claptrap and mere shouting, being essentially a reserved adolescent, recognising few imperatives except those which flowed from the poet and school teacher in him.

His father sensed the truth of his words and stole out to the kitchen to help himself to more live coal for his hookah.

The warmth which came from Maqbool's physique drew Noor to him more ardently than she might, at this age, have been drawn to any lover. Her face glowed as she removed the empty cups from before the guests and poured tea for the newcomers. Then she saw Maqbool's cup lying full of cold tea.

'But,' she said with her own small voiced humour now that father was out of audible distance. 'Your cup is full to overflowing!'

'Oh, Saki,' Maqbool repeated the hackneyed phrase of poetry. 'Bring me a new hot cup of salt tea...' And he smiled at her, even as he turned to Juma, Qadri and Saleem and Mahmdoo.

They warmed to him and turned to him, expecting him to speak.

He looked at them and then began, eloquently:

'All the way to Srinagar I was obsessed by the thought of writing a poem on the terrors of death. But when I got there I saw so much life, so much of life that my fears fell away from me!...It is a question of faith, of belief in ourselves. And in the struggle...And then we can hope to be free...I went through all kinds of moods on the road. I lived through the moods of the people...I thought of their resignation before Allah. But something in me could not accept, though I was spiritless enough, until I saw the people of Srinagar...Then the spirit came into me. And all my being rose in protest against the evil which has been thrust upon us...Now we cannot ignore the sincere faith which the people of Srinagar have put in us—people of Baramula. They expect us to hold out...I know that death is not an amusing thing. And I realise that it may be difficult here. And then, at the end— it won't be like a fairy tale life, happy ever after...But we will still have to struggle. We will have to suffer, and...But that is how we grow.

There was a knock at the door downstairs. This time mother being away, Noor looked out of the window. A whole group of Pathans was there, shouting:

'That bandit Maqbool is up there? Send him down! The son of a donkey! He has given us the slip twice!'

Noor returned from the window, pale and speechless.

'Go and hide,' she said to Maqbool.

By this time his mother and father had gone, running to the windows, while Juma, Qadri, Saleem Bux, and Mahmdoo, got up to take cover.

'Maqbool is not here,' his father lied.

'Open the door!'

'Go away,' Maqbool's mother shrieked.

And she was answered back with profanities.

Mahmdoo came forward and, detaching the fainting Noor from Maqbool, thrust the boy away, saying: 'Run, if you can...go...somewhere...'

The shrewd glance in Mahmdoo's eyes contrasted with the vulnerable tenderness in his voice:

'Go, go...'

'Go away and hide,' whispered Juma.

Maqbool passed his hand over Noor's forehead and looked around desperately. Then, with a jerk of his head, he had decided:

'I will go to the haystack,' he said to Mahmdoo.

'I am coming with you,' said Gula.

'Gula!' Mahmdoo snarled at his son.

But his son had already gone ahead towards the kitchen and waited there to follow Maqbool.

'The only way out is from the rooftop,' Noor said opening her eyes wide. 'Come, I will show you...'

And she got up to go and show her brother, but collapsed to hear heavy steps behind her. The Pakistanis had broken the door downstairs, and were rushing up when Maqbool mounted the steps to the loft of the house from which the window led to the rooftop.

As the sentries came into the sitting room, holding the confectioner Mahmdoo before them, they shouted.

'Where is he? Son of the Devil!...Identify him!'

The man waved his head emptily.

'Rooftop, rooftop!' Noor was moaning in Kashmiri. 'Maqbool hurry away to the rooftop...'

'What does she say?' one of the sentries queried, his red beard glowing like fire.

The confectioner could not speak. But even against his will, his eyes roamed towards the direction where Maqbool had gone.

'The swine, he has given us the slip again. Follow him...Up there! ...It seems he has gone there...'

Maqbool crouched on the precarious edge of the sloping roof of his father's house to survey the position. It would be best to get on to the flat roofs of the houses at the end of the lane and then jump off from there to the fields.

Before he had decided to do this, however, he heard steps coming up the loft. So there was no time to pause and think. He must run for it.

A strange stillness was in his soul. Then panic. His heart drummed. And in front of him he could see the hazards of treading on the tin gutter into which the wooden roof ended. Ten yards of it, before he could reach the first flat roof of the house of the carpenter Akbar. He took the chance.

Crashing of old tin bending under his feet...Crackling of dead leaves...And crunch-crunch of the wooden supports.

The sunlight from the even blue sky guided him in a half playful mood. The odds were that either the tin would give way, and he would fall to his death; or that his pursuers would snipe at him and pick him off, because they were such wonderful marksmen. Or that he would get past the width of his own house onto Akbar's roof.

He found himself getting to the first objective.

As he had half expected, a bullet rang through behind him, just missing his left arm.

He must be bearing a charmed life, for the fire had come almost from thirty yards away.

He wriggled, in spite of himself, feeling he had been shot, though he knew he was still alive.

This made him turn his face to the small window of the loft, and he saw that the sniper was the sentry to whom he had spoken at the confectioner's shop.

He ducked his head behind the projection of the sloping roof and waited for the next move.

Only foul mouthed abuse. And the challenge: 'Come out!'

A prolonged moment.

Apparently the sentry was trying to decide whether he should follow him or adopt some other strategy.

This gave Maqbool time to measure the distance from Akbar's roof to the house at the end of the lane. About a hundred and fifty yards...

He would have to go exposed on roofs and walls. And the next bullet may get him.

He would wait.

'Surround all the houses!' the Pakistanis were shouting. 'And shoot him!'

From the cover which he had taken, it was three yards to the thick wall of Akbar Khan's house. He breathed deeply and tried to get his nerve back.

Instinctively, he lifted the lapel of his shirt to offer a target.

The shot inevitably followed. He had reckoned on five seconds before the sentry could reload.

So he darted towards the wall.

Another bullet coursed down, by him.

There was no escape. He jumped into the sloping roof of the verandah of Akbar Khan's house. Then, without pause, he leapt into the courtyard.

Shrieks...Shouts...Weeping...

But he was set for his objective—the door.

He unlocked the latch and emerged into the lane.

The pursuers had all entered the hall of his own house and the coast was clear.

He ran.

Panting, almost exhausted, his hands grazed badly, he took the curve of the lane, cleanly, almost as a master sprinter. His eyes were nearly blind with the smoke of confusion. His heart beat like the drum of tribesmen, speaking his death knell with each beat. He moaned involuntarily.

Then a barrage of rifle fire opened up behind him. Bullets whizzed past. Obviously, they had come down from his father's house. Not too near yet. But they might catch up with him.

One cartridge went into the side of a door ahead, into old Rajba's house.

Shouts.

They must be following him now.

He leapt past the projection by Zooni's, the weaver woman's house.

He skipped over the hens, which went fluttering before him, cackle, cackle.

Silence.

Again shouts, abuse and challenges.

He couldn't tell who was encouraging him to run and who was asking him to stop.

His mother must be weeping, his sister must have fainted... 'Thanks be to Allah!' his father must be saying...

Allah! Where was Allah? Why was He—always against the innocents?...There would be no salvation unless the religion of fate went by the board and the soul became alive?...Noor's face was like a crumpled flower before his forehead—as she lay helpless!...And his mother's drawn face, uglied by fear...at the back of his head. But his father's face did not appear! Anyhow, how could God punish them so?

The uprush of feelings made for slowness.

He pulled himself together, looked back and saw his pursuers running up, nearly overpowering him.

That moment of the vision of his enemies became a prolonged agony—so clear was the picture of heads and torsos, with rifles pressing forward.

He put all his will into the race to get away.

Another barrage of fire.

One bullet at his heels.

He jumped.

It would be safer to run.

Perhaps they didn't want to kill him outright. That was why they were shooting at his feet.

After he had jumped up and down rubbish heap, his right foot fell in the large greasy puddle of an open drain and had slipped on the slime.

He fell headlong.

What a stupid thing to do! The fellows must be right on him.

He heaved himself from where he lay and stood up.

The advance guard of the pursuers was on him.

Hitting him with the rifle ends, shouting abuse and filth in their broken speech, slapping his face, and thrusting their fisticuffs into his sides, they pulled him from side to side, slapped him again and pushed him forward, till he fell.

They dragged him up and, supporting his sinking form, pushed him forward again, the froth of anger in their shouting, crazed mouths.

The Pakistanis took him to the courtyard of an old caravanserai, which had been used, until their descent upon the town, as stables-cum-residential quarters by the tongawallahs of Baramula.

The dirty, bare courtyard was congested with a horde of tribesmen, who sat drowsily on string charpais, leaning on their bedrolls
and gossiping, as the hookah gurgled in their midst. Most of the
ferocious men stared somnolently at the prisoner as he came in,
ahead of the rifle points of his captors. Maqbool felt so selfconscious
that he did not raise his eyes and went blindly forward.

'A Kafir!' one of the guards announced to his brethren.

For a moment, the hubble-bubble did not gurgle anymore, as all
eyebrows were raised towards the victim. Then some horses, tied to
halters at one end of the stables, neighed in succession, as though
they were sensitive to Maqbools' plight. And the congeries of men
began to pass comments to each other.

Maqbool felt the strong tang of the dung that had been scattered
by the horse's hoofs into the courtyard and he noticed huge flies
buzzing on the refuse.

As his attention was distracted, a tall lanky man, with a cartridge
belt slung from his left shoulder to the right side of his waist, came
over and accosted him.

'Oh, do you not value your life—that you defy us?'

Maqbool felt the impulse to be histrionic and answer back, but
he restrained himself.

His captors made what sounded like a report in a staccato speech
to the tall fellow, who gave some orders to the guards. As a result
of this exchange, his captors pushed him towards the little door of
a cell.

'The orders of Zaman Khan,' one of the guards bawled. 'You will
remain here till Sardar Khurshid Anwar comes to decide your fate.'

Maqbool felt a tremor of relief at the thought of being out of their
reach for a while, if even for a little while. He willingly went forward,
feeling the mouths of the rifles still digging into his back. At length
Zaman Khan advanced, unlatched the iron latch from the hook on
the panel of the rather battered old style door, and flung it open. One

of the captives viciously kicked him from behind, so that he nearly fell headlong into the dungeon, but was saved by the end of a huge bedstead which occupied half the room. An instinctive groan escaped him:

'This will make you into a believer, infidel!' said the guard who had kicked him.

Zaman Khan gave further orders even as he closed the door and fastened the latch in its place.

Maqbool's heart pounced fiercely in spite of his will to suffer what was coming, as the inevitable punishment for his rebel's pride.

In the darkness of the narrow, cavernous Mughal style cell, apparently the home of a tongawallah from the broken leather straps which hung on the pegs on the wall, Maqbool came face to face with his own fears.

He seated himself on the bed, his legs dangling from the perch.

All kinds of thoughts rushed through him. What would his parents be thinking? To be sure, his mother must be weeping, his father sullen and angry, and his sister sad and shedding tears in secret as was her habit. If only he could have been allowed to talk to them at length, to comfort them and to tell them that he had decided to fight it out and die, he would have been content.

But these barbarians had pushed him out. Strange that their slogan was 'Allah ho Akbar!' As he was not a Muslim at all, but only born a Muslim, he need not be shocked, he felt. He had not said the Friday prayers for a long time—no prayers at all since the last Id day, and that was also because there was the feast of sweet vermicelli to follow the morning's ritual in the mosque. He recalled that his mother had asked him to keep at least one fast as a token during the holy month of Ramzan, but he had always laughed away her pleas and said that, as a political agitator, he kept so many enforced fasts, forgetting to eat while wandering from village to village...So the raiders were, after all, being just, from their point of view. To them, it was 'jehad', a holy war, in which all the defenders, and their friends, were infidels who must be destroyed...There was something terrible about this singlemindedness, which drove people to the extremes of brutality without a stirring of their consciences...because he himself would have had doubts before killing people.

In the gloom of the cell, however, such self righteousness seemed only a way of consoling the heart.

Apart from the terror that impinged on his consciousness from every side, the low ceiling, made of rough, wooden planks, over which hung heaps of the tongawallahs' belongings, all covered with black soot of hearth fires, weighed him down.

He saw a cockroach steadily advancing between the planks and he realised that there must be other insects about in the cell, possibly scorpions and rats, and even a snake. His eyes wandered across the dirty surface of the string bed and he was sure that there would be bugs in it. The instinct for the clean life that had always made him recoil back from the disarray of his own home and the squalor in the huts of the poor he visited, assailed him, and his soul shrank at the realisation that if he had to stay here for the night the insects would certainly creep over his body.

Suddenly, he felt that his own clothes were sodden and grimy and torn, and a kind of nausea arose in his mouth, which was partly aroused by the acrid stink of the atmosphere and partly from the thirst for water which possessed him, as also from self disgust.

As he became aware of his thirst, this feeling began to overpower all the rest. He smacked his tongue to quench the thirst, only to find that the nausea increased with the licking.

His eyes explored the gloom of the cell for the pitcher of water that he imagined must be there. And, now, used to the gloom, he traced the curve of a vessel by the oven. He dashed forward and found a glazed earthen cup covering the pitcher in the corner. Impetuously, bending the pitcher on one side, he filled the cup and drank the water, only discovering, as he did so, that the liquid was stale. Then, suddenly, he felt the urge to pass water. This awkward but natural urge seemed to be almost the final humiliation. He was confused and embarrassed by it, and began to sense the poignancy of the absurd situation, which was like the awful predicament he had faced as a child in school once when the schoolmaster would not listen to his plea and he had done it in his salwar.

After a moment's hesitation, and a few circular steps in the middle of the room, he became convinced that the only dignity lay in defying his own self respect, and going to a corner in the dark.

When he had gone through the disgust aroused by the foetid atmosphere, he sat back on the bed, a little calmer, though still with the lingering horror against squalor, inside him.

The absence of any way out of room cleared his conscience. And he had the momentary illusion of being born again, though, immediately, he met the fact of frustration, the anxiety which had always seemed to him to prevail on every curve of his life on which his fate always seemed suspended in the air.

He had the apperception that the verdict of Khurshid Anwar would result in his being strung up in the courtyard of the square, his blood would be clotted on the earth amid the dung of the stables, his body drained of life, all looking so horrible that no one would be able to look at it. He felt he would accept that, if only to be out of this dark chamber. Only, perhaps his sister Noor would come and see the carcass hanging up there—and tears of self pity came into his eyes. And he felt he must at least write her a final message.

His eyes now explored for the light. And, instinctively, he went towards the chinks in the door. By rivetting his eyes about an inch or two away from the line of light he could perhaps write.

He sat down on the earth, resting his back on the door. The light was so thin, he would have to adjust himself sideways.

He felt for his notebook and pencil in the pocket of his tunic and found it was there. For a while, his mind meandered in the many dimensions of the darkness before him, in gradations of vague feelings and the confusion of the unknown experiences yet to come. Then he had the feeling of Noor's long plaits of hair, the way he used to pull them to tease her, to be affectionate to her. And with the feel of the plaits, came the memory of her hands, as they lay dropping on the pillow in her sleep, the swift eager movements of her limbs in the kitchen and the virgin's tenderness in her eyes. He began to scribble:

'My little sister, Noor, we shall not see each other.'

The act of writing with the little pencil in the light of the chink in the dark relaxed his spirit and he persisted.

Love for her flowed out of him on paper in inchoate words of panic and confusion.

Time had been more or less destroyed for him while he wrote to his sister, because he deliberately expected the worst to happen. But during the long wait for something to happen, he tried to imagine that, beyond him, life was going on. And when he knew that this was so, he was full of envy for those who were still alive. He ached to be there with them.

Then, suddenly, there was hubbub in the courtyard, and through the chink of the door, he saw Khurshid Anwar arrive at the head of a little procession, with little round Ahmed Shah leading the train.

The tribesmen in the courtyard got up and bowed, taking their hands to their foreheads to the accompaniment of salutations.

'Where is the traitor Sherwani?' asked Ahmed Shah stepping forward.

Tall Zaman Khan pointed to the cell.

'Arrange a charpai for Khurshid Sahib,' Ahmed Shah said. 'We will try the infidel here and now.'

Some of the soldiers who had been seated on a bedstead near the cell, along with Zaman Khan, in the capacity of watchmen, scattered away, thus leaving a little clearing before the charpai.

Ahmed Shah ran a little caper and, spreading a blanket on the bedstead, smoothed it for Khurshid Anwar to sit upon.

Meanwhile, Zaman Khan proceeded towards the cell, and, unlatching the door, faced Maqbool Sherwani, who had been waiting, with his eyes glued to the chinks in the door.

'Chalo!' Zaman Khan shouted. And then he called three soldiers to come and receive him.

Maqbool's heart, the troubled heart, was beating in spite of himself. He anticipated the worst. And though he had seen his judges come into the courtyard, the suspense was terrible.

The three warders dragged him out, then pushing the muzzles of their rifles into him, they thrust him forward before Khurshid Anwar's improvised court.

The interrogation began without much formality, with a broadside from Ahmed Shah, who strutted about in his self appointed role of public prosecutor.

'Oh, Kafir? Are you still unrepentant?'

Maqbool was dumb at the effrontery of this man, who seemed so anxious to please his new masters. His mind, deadened by the time he had spent in the cell, had not yet got used to the light.

He could not comprehend the process by which a person, supposedly human, could suddenly become a turncoat. He vaguely ascribed the change in Ahmed Shah's attitude to ambition and greed, and, instinctively, he knew these to be the compensation which the little round man required for his lack of physical height.

He sat down on his haunches, instead of answering his ex-friend's questions.

Ahmed Shah advanced in a fury and kicked him, so that Maqbool fell back.

Dazed by the assault, the victim just watched the lawyer, still unable to believe that the thread of connection between the two

Kashmiris should break so completely through the change in political allegiances. Somehow, he could not believe in the scene in which he was involved. He had the hallucination of being in hell. And they all seemed like the angels of Gabriel—frightening monsters. He despised them all, more even than they hated him. And in his heart he was free of them, from the strength of what he believed to be his larger sympathies as against their crude insults. The combination of this belief, and the strange itch of irreverence against the chosen race of the Muslim brotherhood in his limbs, almost made him turn his face away.

But he controlled himself from expressing his disgust against the farce of this trial and sat up, surveying his tormentors from the corners of his reddened eyes, blinking every now and then, as though to adjust himself to the solid reality of Khurshid Anwar and the soldiers before him, and the antics of Ahmed Shah, the solid round pillar of the new society. He felt angry as a lion watching the incomprehensible feats of his tormentors who were twisting his tail, as it were in a circus.

At last the oracle spoke through the sharp, clear Punjabi voice of Khurshid Anwar:

'Answer the questions which are going to be put to you. Otherwise we shall have to extort your confession by other means!... And, if even now you repent and realise that you were born a Muslim, and not a Kafir, we will forgive you! Zaman Khan, stand there by him—and—'

Ahmed Shah cut into Khurshid Anwar's utterance:

'Sardar Khurshid Anwar is being generous to you in the hour of our victory. Tonight our army will be in Srinagar. So I give you the chance to recant. Repeat after me: "I give up my membership of the Kashmir National Conference..."'

Maqbool's nerves had not quite recovered from the shock of his physical humiliation by the Pathan tribesmen who had chased him in the village, when the verbal threats were hurled at him in quick succession by the supreme judge and the prosecutor. He was making up his mind to speak, but his reactions were delayed by his physical condition.

'Zaman Khan!' shouted Ahmed Shah.

'Answer oh—Kafir!' Zaman Khan called, even as he bent over Maqbool and slapped him.

The leopard in Maqbool made him turn after he had reeled under the blow, and his eyes and face glowed with rage. And yet, from underneath the surface layers of his mind, he felt the futility of anger against these performing puppets. He had heard of such rough justice in the old British days of the 'Quit India Movement', when Jayaprakash had been tortured in Lahore jail, and of the tortures in the concentration camps of Nazi Germany, but he had never thought that it would happen again after the world war finished—not in the backwaters of Kashmir.

'You can kill me without all this,' he spoke after all. 'Why do you want to prolong the farce?'

'Khurshid Sahib was being generous to you!' roared Ahmed Shah. 'He wanted to give you a last chance! But you are an ungrateful wretch! A treacherous slave of the Hindu Maharaja and his accomplice Nehru!...Answer me, will you or will you not recant?'

Maqbool was fascinated by the twisting mouth of the rolly polly. He watched the stiffening small boulder-like legs of Ahmed Shah under the fat torso. He saw the rigid stern hand of the lawyer raised in admonition. And he realised that it was no use saying anything in answer to this dummy, all wood and rag. He just stared like an idiot at the automaton.

'Answer me?' shrieked Ahmed Shah, frustrated.

'What do you want to know?' Maqbool said, afraid that a gesture from the prosecutor to Zaman Khan, and the watchdogs with their rifles behind him, would assault him again. Somehow the prolonged physical humiliations seemed worse to him than the direct blow of death, because of his inability to answer back.

Encouraged by the prisoner's response, Ahmed Shah began to hurl his questions on him:

74

'You went to Srinagar some days ago and came back to conduct sabotage against the liberation army of our Muslim brethren in Baramula? Give me the names of your collaborators in Srinagar and Baramula.'

The prisoner could not help grinning stupidly at Ahmed Shah's histrionic manner.

'This is no laughing matter! Answer me? What have you been doing since yesterday when you returned? Whom have you been seeing? Give me full details.'

Maqbool stared at the prosecutor with a set and impassive face.

Ahmed Shah outstared him and shouted:

'How many people have you contacted since last night?'

Maqbool looked from face to face and then withdrew his eyes, because the whole court seemed like a shaken kaleidoscope before his dizzy brain.

'If you will not answer, Zaman Khan will make you disgorge the facts in his own way!' threatened Khurshid Anwar. 'If you value your life, be a good man, an honest Muslim, and answer!'

'You are pro-Bharat still, are you not?' shouted Ahmed Shah.

'So were you once!' answered Maqbool as though speaking aloud to himself.

'But I have repudiated the traitors who have sold Kashmir to the Maharaja and to Nehru! I spit in the faces of all your leaders! I shall try them for their crimes against the people of Kashmir as soon as our armies enter Srinagar!...And you need not expect any mercy from me, because you were once known to me!...I could have saved your life if you had recanted. But you dare to insult me!...'

'Never mind,' said Khurshid Anwar, knowing that his lackey was reacting stupidly. 'Don't let us waste time? It will soon be time for the evening prayers...Proceed...' And he looked at the reddening western sky, where the sun was going down.

'You are pro-Nehru! And your leaders in Srinagar are pro-Bharat! All of you have united and called in the Indian army to desecrate the sacred soil of Muslim Kashmir, whose people want to unite with their brethren in Pakistan. And you and your friends are helping the Indian army. Admit it?—That you are a traitor?'

Maqbool's eyes had also followed Khurshid Anwar's to the western sky. What was more, he felt that he heard a distant rumbling on the horizon. And his attention was distracted, so that he heard but did not listen to Ahmed Shah's fateful indictment. His prejudice against the lawyer made him unresponsive to the mechanical intensity of the prosecutor's voice. He felt remote.

'Come to your senses! Rape sister,' shouted Khurshid Anwar. 'Do you not value your life?'

'I value my sister's honour more than my life!' Maqbool answered. 'So please do not abuse me like that.'

'Insolent swine!' shouted Ahmed Shah. 'You are persisting in your treachery and don't realise that a word from Mr. Khurshid Anwar—and Zaman Khan will finish you off!...Recant your treacherous stand or I shall have no option but to ask the court to pronounce judgement on you!...'

The enormity of the prosecutor's abuse suffocated him. He inhaled a deep breath, swallowed some saliva, drank his anger and remained silent.

'Speak and ask forgiveness from Khurshid Sahib!' Ahmed Shah roared.

Maqbool believed in his honest face as his answer and, though realising that there was no way of communicating a point of view which was the opposite of his judge's, he nevertheless ought to breathe out the words.

'Truth has no voice,' he began by chewing the words in the bitter froth in his mouth to himself, so that his lips did not open and no voice could be heard. Only his will flourished for the while. 'I have no face,' he said. 'I have no speech. I say to myself: This land, which gave birth to me, this land which is like a poem to me—how shall I explain my love for it to you? From out of its valleys there has risen for centuries anguish of torture...And we were trying to emerge from oppression to liberate our mother, because we know her each aching caress!...You have come and fouled her! How could any of us stand by and not protest?...All invaders behave like that. And I can understand and forgive the mercenaries. But I cannot forgive your treachery—Ahmed Shah.'

Ahmed Shah rushed up towards him after contemplating his tight-mouthed presence for a prolonged moment, kicked him furiously, so that Maqbool fell back again.

'I demand immediate death for him! He is a self-confessed rebel! And unrepentant!'

'Thief accusing the sheriff!' Khurshid Anwar mumbled with a half guilty tone in his voice, because he had, in spite of himself, been moved by Maqbool's defence. Then he assumed the theatrical manner of the judge and said: 'If a prisoner cannot recant then there is only one thing for him!...'

He got up with a certain deliberation which showed that he felt unequal to the task of pronouncing the sentence, and turned his face away.

'Zaman Khan, put him up there and shoot him!' said Ahmed Shah rushing towards the tall warder. 'What do you say, Khurshid Sahib? You have to give the final order!...'

Khurshid Anwar nodded, but said: 'I must ask the sanction of the higher authorities before carrying out the sentence...Zaman Khan, keep him in custody for the night in the same cell...'

Zaman Khan leant over and tapped Maqbool on the shoulders, asking him to get up.

Maqbool obeyed the behest and stood vacuously, unable to think or feel, though his heart had begun to throb again out of the instinctive love of dear life. The sense of hearing himself, a puppet among the puppet shapes of his tormentors, crept into him, with a sense of the futility of ignoble existence, he moved towards the cell of the stables where Zaman Khan led him.

Restored to the darkness of the cell, Maqbool was partially relieved, though, in another part of his being, he wished that they had ended his agony by executing him there and then, after the summary trial, rather than consign him to this suspense again. And yet, somewhere in a corner, there lurked the hope of a reprieve.

His nerves were worn out by the violence of the interrogation and he felt tired and lay down on the bed.

With the nightfall outside, the gloom of the room increased and, though his eyes got used to the dark, he could not see much.

He tried to sleep, but waves of delirium ran through him, making his violent heart drum against his will; and there was an ache at the back of his head and on his temples. He wanted to reach out among the flashing stars before his shut eyes for the reasons of this disturbance. But his mind seemed to have been emptied out of all content, because a numbness spread from inside him, enveloping him and making him part of the inert darkness around him. It was as if he had been suddenly paralysed and left listless and cold like a frozen jelly. And, a peculiar chilliness seemed to be growing within him till he felt exhausted and half dead. Sheer physical fatigue made him listless.

As he felt like a carcass, he turned over on his side, hoping that the change of position would enable him to sleep. But the weight of the nullity in him suspended over his body in a kind of hopelessness, which was due both to ennui and to the dim sense of coming end. He sighed and then smacked his lips and tried to shake off the morbid depression which lay inertly on his limbs.

There was the sound of distant rumbling of guns, a heavy zoom which lasted quite a few minutes.

He wondered if his oppressors had finished the trial quickly, because there was a heavy battle going on and they wanted to be on guard. Had the Indian army come and the heavy zooms emanated from their guns? Elated at this thought, he then thought it would be a miracle to expect that he would benefit from it, in this obscure cell in the stables of the tonga drivers of Baramula. No one would come looking for him here. And yet, perhaps, his parents might apprise them of what had happened, and they might come. His sister would certainly insist on their searching for him. And he felt a quiver of tenderness go through him at the prospect of being found and liberated by her.

The guns ceased to bark, however, and the forebodings that had possessed him earlier again became so powerful and black that the spark of hope was extinguished.

There was nothing for it, but to turn upside down and descend into the pit of darkness, for perchance, sleep might come into his eyes.

The ghastliness of the nightmare was increased by the fact that in his half sleep Maqbool could also feel the dark walls of the cell to be eloquent. He was carrying his own head on the palm of his left hand, while he held a sword in the right. The familiar shapes of his mother and sister stood weeping among the crowd in the gallery...Exhausted by the panic of his flight before the pursuing police, he was, however, still brandishing his sword. Before him now was a well from which emerged the alabaster effigy of a woman with bullet holes in the belly and on the lovely neck. The image fell, with a ringing as of a hundred bells, and there was a thud, and secret hidden forms emerged from a graveyard and brushed past him. And great lidless eyes roved wildly searching into his eyes. He flew away with all the power in his limbs from those ogling eyes. And, in a second, he had travelled through many spheres in the courtyard of a mosque, in which crosses stood broken over little mounds of graves. As he was wondering how crosses could have come to be fixed on graves in a mosque, he became conscious of the presence of some raiders on the plinth of the mosque, shrieking, 'Allah ho Akbar!' and calling upon him, Maqbool, to surrender. Among them was the face of Khurshid Anwar, who was shouting in Punjabi, while

Ahmed Shah appeared from behind the crowd and lifted him and fixed him against the sky, before a giant with a big white beard who looked like God. All his ambitions and his peculiar determinations seem to slither down from his body and fall away, as though he was already dead, the pale ghost of himself—about to be put into the grave...But, before he could be exalted to the presence of the Omnipotent judge, or consigned to a pit, he felt that he was suspended in midair and—

Opening his eyes in the dark, dripping with sweat, he sensed the zooming of deafening artillery and machine gun fire.

He was sure that there was a battle raging in Baramula itself. He waited for the firing to stop. There was a brief lull. But the zooming of the big guns began again.

He tried to remember bits of his nightmare, but could only see the great bearded image of the Omnipotent judge.

He inhaled a deep breath. Filming into his brain, over the glistening tissues of light in his eyes, he could see more snippets of humans wafting about. Waves of fear coursed through him.

For five minutes, he lay embroiled in the vaporous atmosphere of his dim apprehensions. Then he heard the door being thrust open.

He sat up in a panic.

Zaman Khan and the two sentries were on him.

He felt the tight throated protest of his dream arise towards his larynx, and his mouth opened, but no sound came out.

The soldiers lifted him and dragged him out.

He looked at them with a terrible curiosity, almost as though he was imploring them to tell him what they meant to do to him. But he could not see their faces clearly and his gaze became fixed in a deathly stare in front of him.

The tall Pathan Zaman Khan walked ahead of Maqbool, while the other two warders followed behind him.

80

Strange and amorphous were his sensations now, bordering upon the hope that, perchance, the orders had come for him to be released. Then the apprehension of the final shooting. There could be no other solution awaiting him, since they had dragged him out, in the middle of the night. His heart was pounding against his will.

He heard Zaman Khan say in a loud whisper. 'He is here, sire!'

And Maqbool saw the contours of Ahmed Shah, standing in the courtyard, mobile and seemingly agitated.

A hot anger surged up in him at this man's persistence in seeing him tortured, and he wanted to shout at him for all his falseness. But the noise of the bombardment drowned his fury, even as it made the lawyer more nervy.

'Quick, Zaman Khan!' Ahmed Shah shouted.

'Traitor!' began Ahmed Shah facing Maqbool. 'Lift your eyes high to Allah! Your end has come!...And, then, turning to Zaman Khan, he continued: 'I shall count one, two, three. At three the warders must shoot!'

Zaman Khan communicated the order to his men. And, adjusting himself to his full height, with his hands on his hips, he looked in the direction of Ahmed Shah.

Maqbool suppressed a sigh at the end of which the despairing cry Hai Ma! formed itself, and got swallowed up in the dryness of his throat. He stared at the deranged round face of Ahmed Shah, wondering why he had never been able to gauge the meanness, and hatred in this warped man. He closed his eyes and tried to conjure up the image of his sister in his mind, but her figure failed to arise.

Ahmed Shah shouted the dread numbers.

Zaman Khan repeated the order.

At the utterance two shots rang out.

There was only a blurr before Maqbool's eyes, followed by waves of darkness. And his body collapsed in a heap—the blood shooting up as from a fountain.

For a moment Ahmed Shah's eyes blinked. Then he dug his feet solidly into the earth and ordered Zaman Khan:

'Lift his corpse and tie it to the pole behind him. And write the word 'Kafir' on his shirt with his own blood. The whole population of Baramula should know that treachery is punishable only with death!'

The glint in his eyes was liquid under the red pupils. And Zaman Khan seemed mesmerised by the orders, as he began to do faithfully what he had been told.

As Ahmed Shah's inflated body moved, his shrunken soul quivered involuntarily to see the flashes of artillery fire over Baramula. He wanted to mumble a prayer from the Koran, but words would not come to his mouth. In a panic, he shouted, as though to fill his craven soul with confidence:

'Allah ho Akbar!'

The next day, when the Indian troops entered Baramula, they found almost half the town raised to the ground. And, as they combed the streets and houses, they entered the Mughal caravanserai and found the body of Maqbool Sherwani tied to a wooden pole in the stables, with the word 'Kafir' written on the lapel of his shirt...The body looked almost like a scarecrow, but also like that of Yessuh Messih on the cross. As they went through his pockets for a possible diary, they found a wad of papers, which were obviously a letter he had written.

'My sister, Noor, we shall not see each other again...They have brought me here to the stables in the ruined caravanserai and put me in a dark room. And though, at first, the verdict was not given, their faces spoke clearly enough of their intentions. "You are a traitor. And

82

you will be tried and shot." As they did not say these words in the beginning, I was not quite certain of my fate. But their faces were not human. And their eyes were withdrawn. And they handled me so roughly that I felt the judgement was clear enough. So I too remained silent and did not ask any questions...What questions can one ask these murderers, who have attacked our country? They consider anyone who defends Kashmir to be a traitor. Surprisingly, my old friend, the lawyer Ahmed Shah, who is a real traitor, both to friendship and to our country, is favoured by them. And they have declared Jehad, a holy war, to save us Muslim brethren from the embrace of the Hindus of India. To confer freedom on us by force seems the sheerest folly. Often in human life, stupidity wins and decency is on the losing side.

'I know that you have always thought of me as somewhat of a hero, Noor. Always there was a light in your big eyes which said so. But, today, I want to write and tell you, so that you can tell everyone that I have never been anything but an aspirant to poetry. All my dreams will remain unfulfilled, because I am going to face death. But here, in our country, the most splendid deeds have been done by people, not because they were great in spirit, but because they could not suffer the tyrant's yoke, and learnt to obey their consciences. And conscience, howsoever dim, is a great force, and is the real source of poetry. For, from the obedience to one's conscience to pity, is but a small step. And pity is poetry and poetry is pity. In our beloved Kashmir today, no one can be human without listening to his conscience, and to the orchestra of feelings without voices which is our landscape. And everyone who listens is being true to our heritage of struggle.

'When I was in Srinagar the other day and was sitting around, trying to decide what to do, whether to stay in the capital or come back to Baramula, to organise the struggle here, I asked the advice, not of a leader, but of a young Punjabi sitting next to me. He said: "No one can advise you. Because it is important in these times, that a man should consult himself. There are Pakistanis who have come to fight in Kashmir, most of them because they were promised loot, but some of them, consciously, because they want to conquer this country and make it part of their 'Pure' state. They, too, these men, are facing the danger of death. And they fight well, at the moment better than we are doing! But that is not heroism. It is just gangster pride. If you choose to go to Baramula, your deed will be heroic, because you will be facing death in the defence of your home, while they are trying to conquer other people's territory. I know what your choice will be..."

'I am writing this to you, because I could not explain to mother and father why I came back. And as you are young, and always had that light of hope in your eyes when you looked at me, I know you will understand why I made the choice I did make. And, some day, you will be able to explain this to our parents. It is better that they should know this, because I should not like to think that they thought I was just impetuous and foolhardy, and because I would not like them to indulge in vague sentimental feelings, about what might have been if I had not come back. Strange, but this is my philosophy of life—I love people!...And I want father and mother to accept this truth from their love for me...

'And now I am a little sad that I always refused mother's advice and did not agree to marry. Because in this she was right. It is foolish not to have children. Life should continue. It should prevail against death. For it is to help life to continue and prevail and flourish in Kashmir that we are suffering and dying...I would have been more contented in facing the future, if there had been growing up, in our household, an heir to my poet's longings and aspirations. If life continues, then death, even sudden death, is as reasonable as birth, or life itself.

'You are the only person to whom I could have written these words. Because you are a young girl with dreams of your own and will soon understand what I am saying. I did not write to father because I know he will say that I exaggerate everything in my "vagabond poet's manner" and he will not understand that raising everything to the highest pitch may be romantic, but it is necessary when death has raised the value of life. And when you are married and have a child, I want you to remember this and let your offspring bear my name. I think your husband will permit this, because I am sure you will choose an enlightened man to be your companion in life...And your child will grow up and work for our lovely land, and through him or her, my spirit will be working for the new life in our country.

'There is hardly any light and I cannot write more.'

Later:

'I am adding some more words: They took me out and tried me. Ahmed Shah demanded my death on the charge that I am a proven traitor. The Pakistani officer is asking his headquarters for confirmation of this sentence. I think the dice is loaded against me on the chess board...I am glad that they have warned me about death. But there is very little doubt left now and suspense would have been more terrible than is this certainty. And, with the certainty of death before me, I can renew my faith in life. I shall love life with the last drop of my blood. And I want you to cherish this love of life, because you are young and will understand this love...I kiss you tenderly on your forehead and on each of your big black eyes.'

● ● ●

IN PRAISE OF DEATH OF A HERO

By Dieter Riemenshneider

In *Death of a Hero*, Anand turns his attention to the meaning of life in general. From this point of view it seems to me *Death of a Hero* is one of the writer's highest achievements. Though the action takes place in India in Kashmir and the hero is an Indian, his problem is only superficially that of a particular historical situation; basically, it is the problem of a man; the confrontation with death because of one's own convictions.

The story itself is extremely simple. Action takes place more in the soul of the hero than in reality. The young Muslim freedom-fighter Maqbool flees Baramula to Srinagar when the Pakistani intruders occupy that place. He is then ordered to return and help the people. He re-enters the town secretly but is soon discovered, pursued and arrested. When asked to give up his membership of the Indian Kashmir National Conference and join his Muslim brethren from Pakistan, he refuses and is shot as a traitor.

Again we are reminded of Ananta in Anand's novel *The Big Heart*, whose life is driven to the same extreme situation. But Ananta's death occurs tragically. At the crucial moment he is not aware of his own sacrifice. In Maqbool, the idea of death, however, plays an important role right from the beginning of his assignment. In fact, at all stages he is acutely aware of his own fears and weaknesses. He also doubts whether his activities are meaningful in any way. He is seized repeatedly by fear. And at one point even considers going back. When he is arrested all his willpower cannot suppress his fear. 'Maqbool's heart pounced fiercely in spite of his will to suffer what was coming, as the inevitable punishment for his rebel's pride.'

Connected with this instinctive response is his questioning for the meaning and sense of his mission. The meetings with those he wants to unite are disheartening. Though the cookshopwallah Mahmdoo is on his side, he cannot convince him to assist him. Maqbool asks himself, 'What was the use of his going to Baramula to rally people, if he could not convince this man. And a little later, 'But what exactly could he do? He could only sound opinion, tell them the news of the imminent help from India and wait.'

Because of his own uncertainty Maqbool's arguments sound more like mechanically repeated opinions of others. But as soon as he really faces the 'other side', particularly his former friends of the revolutionary movement who have now joined the Pakistanis, he suddenly understands the meaning of his instructions. He realizes the evil done by intruders, their greed, violence, murder and looting under the pretence of liberating the Muslims from the slavery of the Hindus. Religion, Maqbool discovers, serves as a vehicle to commit atrocities. His experience has now taught him that his arguments in favour of human values like liberty, justice and reason do not lack a basis. His defence of these values during a discussion with his enemies is no mere textbook statement but has become a part of his own self: 'We must fight against the violent destroyers of life with violence. There is such a thing as goodness and honesty—as there is evil and lies...Ours is the human response of pity for those whom they have despoiled!...'

The more Maqbool identifies himself with his views, the calmer the way he faces the prospect of death. All the abuses and tortures of his opponent cannot change him. But for all his strength and endurance Maqbool never becomes superhuman. He is courageous and honest not only to others but also to himself. He admits his fears and feels envious of those who are living outside the prison-cell. Nor does he exaggerate the part he is acting: 'The sense of hearing himself, puppet among the puppet shapes of his tormentors, crept into him, with a sense of the futility of the whole thing.' Maqbool attains the status of greatness because in his heart he remains humble.

The novel ends with the letter Maqbool had written to his sister. And now Anand succeeds in expressing what he means by his idea of man. There is no break between the life and death of the main character and the message he has to communicate. Anand has used a simple device, which does not destroy the unity of the novel. Thus the artist and message-giver finally find a way to put forward their different approaches without interfering with each other. *Death of a Hero* is not only Anand's deepest probe into the potentiality of man but also his most satisfying artistic achievement.

Epitaph for Maqbool Sherwani is the harrowing true story of a poet who was crucified by wild Pathan terrorists sent to capture Kashmir, a few days after the Maharaja's accession to free India in 1947.

Rising above the dangers of his return to his hometown, Baramula, on the behest of Sheikh Muhammad Abdullah and his patriotic council, who had preferred liberty in secular India rather than join Pak theocracy, Maqbool Sherwani goes through terror, unleashed by mercenary guerillas, to face nightmare of loot and killing of the invaders. Betrayed by the greedy little men who have succumbed to lure of money and power, he is caught after a chase, to face his tormentors. He is shot after a mock trial and leaves behind a tender letter to his sister about his belief in future—of the struggle for hope against despair.

This short novel has been called by an eminent critic as one of Mulk Raj Anand's "highest achievements".

Mulk Raj Anand is a doyen of Indian-English writing. He left metaphysical studies to write novels of the human condition, through his conversion from abstractions to pity for the shunned, after a stay in Mahatma Gandhi's Ashram.

His early novels, *Untouchable* and *Coolie*, are considered classics and have gone into over twenty world languages each. He continues his saga of liberty in his long novel *Seven Ages of Man*.